/50

LUKE SUTTON: AVENGER

By Leo P. Kelley

LUKE SUTTON: AVENGER

LEO P. KELLEY

DOUBLEDAY & COMPANY, INC.

GARDEN CITY, NEW YORK

1983

W

All of the characters in this book
are fictitious, and any resemblance
to actual persons, living or dead,
except for historical personages,
is purely coincidental.

Library of Congress Cataloging in Publication Data

Kelley, Leo P.
Luke Sutton: avenger.

(Double D Western)
I. Title.
PS3561.E388L826   1983   813'.54
ISBN 0-385-18396-8
Library of Congress Catalog Card Number 82–45560

LUKE SUTTON:
AVENGER

CHAPTER 1

Four men, Sutton thought as he sat on the edge of the bed and pulled on his battered black boots.

Three years, he thought.

He stood up and went to the open window. He looked down at the crocuses which were in full bloom, their yellow, white, and lavender blossoms sprinkled like bright spots of paint on the green lawn below him.

Nearly three years had passed, he thought, as he stood musing at the window and the soft spring breeze stirred his straight black hair which covered his ears and the nape of his neck. Three years had passed and three of the four men he had been hunting during that time were as dead as were the years themselves.

He closed his eyes momentarily and drew a deep breath of the early morning air as he thought of the one man he had not yet tracked down.

Adam Foss.

He thought of his brother, Dan. Dead and gone now—murdered nearly three years ago. By four men. Three of whom are also dead now, he thought, because I caught up with them.

He opened his eyes and gazed out over the rooftops of Carson City's houses and commercial buildings. Where was Foss?

He didn't know.

But he knew there would come a day and he hoped it would be soon, hoped it might be tomorrow, even today, when he would stand face to face with Adam Foss and Foss would know with a terrible certainty that he had reached the end of whatever trail he had been traveling until the moment of that fatal meeting.

Sutton's lips formed a grim line. I'll find Foss, he told himself. I've got to and I will. I want the man. He belongs to me more than he belongs to himself. He felt the all too familiar hatred that was fired by rage well up within him. Foss will die, he thought. I'm going to see to it that he does, just as I've seen to it that the other three died—the three who were with Foss that night when the four of them shot Dan to death and wounded me, leaving me for dead.

The sun rose above the rooftops and its light splashed Sutton's face, causing him to blink and turn away from the window.

"Luke!"

The sound of Eileen Dugan's voice banished the hatred surging within Sutton. He went to the bedroom door and opened it. "I'm coming!" he called out as he went out into the hall and then down the stairs to find her alone in the kitchen. "Where's everybody?" he asked.

"Most men who have livings to earn," Eileen answered, "get an early start else the world will go on without them."

Sutton smiled. "I woke up at dawn as usual. But I must have dozed off again."

"Back in the old country," Eileen said as she began to fry two eggs, "my sainted mother would have switched my behind were I not up well before the sun."

"This is the New World," Sutton remarked, sitting down at the table. "We do things different here. We only switch balky mules and saddle-spooked mustangs. Not pretty women like yourself."

"Blather!" Eileen snapped and turned away.

But not before Sutton saw her smile. "That does look tasty," he said as she placed a plate containing the two eggs and some crisp bacon in front of him. "I'm mighty glad that Mrs. Reardon sees fit to feed her boarders so good."

"I can't abide a hungry man," declared a portly woman as she swept into the kitchen. "A hungry man's a pestering man."

"There's nothing worse than a cranky cowboy," Sutton commented. "He's likely to scare cows and cause a chuckwagon cook to start in on a long string of curses."

"Good day, ma'am," Eileen said to Mrs. Reardon. Then, to Sutton, she said, "You're not a cowboy. You're a blacksmith."

"A blacksmith's helper," he corrected her. "But I've been a cowboy in my time. Might turn into one again someday."

"Girl," said Mrs. Reardon, gesturing, "pour this once-upon-a-time cowboy some coffee to open his eyes and put some starch in his spine."

Eileen promptly did as she had been told and Sutton drank from the cup before remarking, "The crocuses are up. Daffodils'll be sprouting pretty soon."

"Spring's my favorite season of the year," Mrs. Reardon declared as she sat down across from Sutton and poured herself a cup of coffee. "In Ireland spring's like a good snort of John Barleycorn. Spring sets the blood to boiling and the mind to reeling. You two, I take it, are going to the dance at the Grange Hall tonight." She shot swift glances, first at Sutton, then at Eileen.

Eileen blushed.

Sutton grinned. "If the lady hasn't gone and changed her mind on me, we are."

Mrs. Reardon harrumphed, her ample bosom heaving. "She'd be a fool if she did. Any slip of a girl who has a handsome man to pay her mind had best stick to her knitting before some other woman moves in on the territory she's staked a claim to."

Eileen's blush deepened and she busied herself unnecessarily at the stove.

Mrs. Reardon gave Sutton a sharp, inquiring glance. "Are you serious about Eileen, Luke? Are you going to gain a wife and make me lose a hired girl?"

"Now, Mrs. Reardon, that's a question that puts me on a very hot spot," Sutton replied.

"You're a steady man," Mrs. Reardon commented thoughtfully. "But," she quickly added, "you're not a churchgoer and Eileen's Irish and the Church is as important to her as is her very soul."

Sutton finished the last of his breakfast. "It's true that I'm not a churchgoer, Mrs. Reardon. But, if it will ease your heart any, I am Irish."

"Go on with yourself!" Mrs. Reardon exclaimed in disbelief. "With a name like Sutton you're no son of the old sod."

"Well, it's true enough that some of the British are named

Sutton. But so are some Irish. My pa told me we came by our name due to the fact that a long time ago our ancestors were ordered by the British to give up our real names and take other ones—British ones. Somebody in our line took on the name Sutton, which was the name of a British town."

"Let the saints be praised!" cried Mrs. Reardon, beaming at Sutton. Then, turning to Eileen, she crowed, "Did you hear him, girl? Now, did you just? He's an Irishman and all this time I've been thinking he was as British as London itself!"

"I heard him," Eileen said, casting a brief glance in Sutton's direction. "But you know as well as me, ma'am, Luke isn't one to talk much about himself."

"My pa," Sutton said, "fought in the Tithe War when he was little more than a lad. That was long before he crossed the pond and came over here to this country on account of the potato famine. I used to like to hear him tell stories about the great Irish patriots. Men like Daniel O'Connell, the man they called 'the Liberator,' who was born near Cahirciveen in County Kerry, and who fought so hard for Irish Home Rule even though the British arrested him for what he did and charged him with seditious conspiracy."

Eileen had turned from the stove and was staring at Sutton in undisguised amazement. "Glory be to God!" she cried. "I'd no idea—you never would talk about yourself—you didn't like me questioning you. . . ."

"A man, I admit, is made in part by his past," Sutton said slowly, "but it's the here and now that matters most. What he is today—what he does and whether you can respect him— that's what counts in the long run." He met Eileen's gaze.

"Luke speaks the gospel truth, girl!" Mrs. Reardon declared emphatically. "It's not a man's breeding that matters. It's whether he can look other men square in the eye without so much as a blink and whether he can hold his own among them without fear or fawning. Luke can," she concluded, just as emphatically.

"I know," Eileen said, her eyes on Sutton. "I think I knew that about him since he first came to board here."

"I'll remember that day till I die," Mrs. Reardon said. "When I first set eyes on him, I thought, oh my, such a striking young man. Looks as pretty as the sun shining on the Lakes of Killarney."

It was Sutton's turn to blush. "Pretty?" He grinned sheepishly.

"You know what I mean," Mrs. Reardon said to him. "If I had been younger—well, Eileen might have had herself some stiff competition, let me tell you, Luke. But no one wants an old widow woman like me. I talk too much and pry more. I'm just an old biddy, it's that pure and simple."

"You're a woman I've found to be both kind and helpful," Sutton said sincerely. "When I first came here, I could only pay you for one week's room and board. But you didn't toss me out on my ear when my week was up."

"I knew you'd find something," Mrs. Reardon said firmly. "I told you then that you would and you did. You're a blacksmith now."

"A blacksmith's helper," Sutton corrected. "And if I don't get myself down to the smithy, Cal Hooper's going to take a switch to me."

"I thought you said things were different in the New World," Eileen remarked impishly. "You said that here people only switched balky mules and saddle-spooked horses."

"Ah, girl, did I go and say that now?" Sutton said, affecting a thick brogue. He shook his head in mock chagrin. "That just goes to show you that you can't put too much faith in what an Irishman says when his tongue gets loose."

He emptied his cup and rose.

Eileen glanced hesitantly in Mrs. Reardon's direction.

Mrs. Reardon waved her away and she followed Sutton to the front door.

"Did you put polish on your dancing shoes?" he asked her.

She nodded and he kissed her lightly on the lips. "To tell you the truth, Eileen, I don't know what you see in a man like me."

"I'll tell you then. I see a man—a tall man—with wide shoulders and almost no hips to speak of. A man with hair the color of crows and eyes as gray as pond ice. I see a man with a straight nose, straighter lips, a broad forehead, and a square chin. I see a man made for making mischief with a girl like me, one who could be easy for a girl to love if only he'd let her come close to him."

Sutton put his arms around her and hugged her to him.

"That's not what I meant about coming close, Luke, and you know it."

"I have to go, Eileen. I'm late."

"Cal Hooper and his switch?"

"Cal Hooper and his switch. The way he swings it, it's enough to make a man smart for days and take his meals standing straight up."

Eileen laughed and Sutton kissed her again before releasing her. He bounded down the steps, turned to wave to her, and then hurried up the street.

Cal Hooper's fourteen-year-old son, Clay, greeted Sutton with a frown as he entered the smithy.

"What's soured you this morning, boy?" Sutton asked him. "You look like a dog that didn't run fast enough after spotting a skunk."

"That horse," Clay answered, pointing to a bay in the nearest stall. "Pa—he's not in yet on account of the gout's got to him again—told me I could have a try at shoeing him. But he won't let me get near him. He belongs to Mr. Emerson."

"Heat up the forge, boy." Sutton went and stood beside the stall, studying the small but sturdy animal inside it. He went around to the front of the stall and looked down at the animal's front feet.

Clay, at the forge, called out, "Mr. Emerson told Pa he

thinks there's something wrong with that horse's feet or legs maybe. He stumbles."

"Who? Mr. Emerson or the horse?"

Clay opened his mouth to reply and then, seeing the grin on Sutton's face, he laughed and picked up the bellows to fan the forge's fire.

Sutton went to the rear of the stall and looked down at the horse's hind legs and feet. Taking a knife from a wooden shelf, he stepped into the stall.

"Watch out, Luke! He might be a biter." Clay came over to the stall and stood outside it, watching Sutton, who went up to the front of the stall and bent over, letting the bay smell him. He carefully avoided looking the horse in the eye. He straightened. Sniffed.

"I smell something," he said, sniffing again. "Coal oil, or I miss my guess."

"You're right," Clay said. "I was trimming the wicks in our lamps last night and spilled some on my shirt."

"There you go, boy. It's no wonder this bay wouldn't let you come up close. He couldn't stand the smell of you. Now my clothes have a horsey smell to them even after they're washed good so this critter maybe thinks I'm a cousin of his so he doesn't get spooked." Sutton reached into the feed bin and picked up a handful of grain. Still not looking directly into the horse's eyes, he let the bay eat the grain he held in the palm of his hand.

"Best thing is to try to make friends—or at least not enemies—with a horse you're about to work on," he told Clay. "Don't look him in the eyes. Sometimes that scares them." Sutton, the grain gone, placed his shoulder against the bay's body. "Let them get to feel you and find out you mean them no harm." He ran a hand lightly over the bay's shoulder and then his hand came to rest against the horse's ribs.

The bay turned its head. It nickered.

Sutton spoke to it in a soft voice, told the animal he was a good boy, a brave boy, whispered that the two of them had some business together and it was about time to be getting on with it—if that was alright with the bay.

He stepped away from the horse and ran a hand down its leg. "Don't grab for a horse's leg," he told Clay, speaking softly. "Come at him slow and easy."

Suddenly the bay reared.

Sutton kept his hand on the horse's leg. As the bay came down, he let his shoulder touch the horse's shoulder. "Keep your hands on him if you can," he said to Clay. "Or your shoulder."

"What if he tries to bite you?" Clay asked. "Or kick you?"

"You can usually tell when a bite or kick's coming. You just have to be nimble, boy. But, if you get bit or kicked, try not to get mad at the horse even if you're hurting. Forget your problems. Think of his. Maybe he's scared. Maybe the last man who handled him was too rough on him and he's wary. Or maybe he's just spoiled rotten. In that case, you're going to have your hands full with him. Best thing to do with a spoiled horse is to throw him down, tie up his legs with a bale of hay between them before you go to work on him. Hand me a clinch cutter, boy, and those shoe tongs."

Sutton, when he had the tools, lifted the bay's front left foot. He placed it between his knees and cut the clinches. He used the shoe tongs to pry up both branches of the shoe. When he had removed the shoe, he pulled a nail that had remained in the wall of the hoof and said, "No wonder this old fellow stumbles."

"Why does he, Luke?"

"Come on over here and take a look, boy."

When Clay had rounded the stall, Sutton said, "See here. This foot's not been trimmed proper. Toe wasn't trimmed enough so his foot angle's broken back."

"Mr. Emerson said he'd had that horse worked on by the best smith in Carson City."

"Point is, he didn't have him worked on by your pa or this wouldn't have happened." Sutton used his knife to trim the wall of the hoof, paying particular attention to lowering the toe so that the horse, once shod, would have a better posture and be less likely to stumble as a result.

The bay leaned against Sutton.

Sutton shifted the position of the foot between his knees but the horse continued to lean heavily against him. He released the hoof and stepped swiftly backward away from the animal.

The bay fell to the ground, barely missing the wall of the stall, and then after thrashing helplessly for a moment, managed to regain its feet.

"What happened?" Clay asked excitedly.

"He's a leaner, looks like, but I'm not about to hold him up. He's not leg-weary or sickly. I reckon now maybe he's learned his lesson. But, just in case he hasn't, hand me that rope hanging over there, boy."

When Clay gave him the looped rope, Sutton wrapped it around the bay's rear left foot and then around the animal's neck, tying it in place so that the horse's foot was raised several inches off the ground.

"He'll keep his mind on staying upright now," Sutton commented. "Now that I've Scotch-hobbled him, I figure he won't be of a mind to lean on me."

He proceeded to hammer out a new shoe, using the horn of the anvil to round the hot metal he was working and the anvil's face for straightening the shoe.

As he finished shaping the shoe, he plunged it and the end of the tongs that held it into a barrel of salt water to cool them. Later, when the shoe was ready, he proceeded to nail it in place on the bay's hoof.

As he was finishing the shoeing, Cal Hooper, leaning on a cane, came into the smithy. Sutton straightened and said, "Morning, Mr. Hooper."

"How many times do I have to tell you to call me Cal, Luke? You got something against my given name?"

"No, sir—Cal."

"That's better," Hooper grumbled.

"Pa," Clay said, "you remember what Mr. Emerson said? About his horse stumbling?"

Hooper waited.

"Luke says the trouble was that whoever shoed him last time didn't trim his toes proper. Luke said his foot angle was broken back."

"You saw to it, Luke?" Hooper asked.

Sutton nodded. "He's all set to go whenever Mr. Emerson sees fit to come for him."

"Good. Now, I got another job for you. I'll help you if this gout that's trying to kill me by inches'll let me. Clay, drag that iron gate over here." As Clay went to the far side of the smithy, Hooper said, "A runaway horse crashed into Miz Lane's fence and the wagon it was hauling bent her gate all out of shape."

"I'll get to work on it right away, Mr.—Cal."

"First, though, you take yourself a look at this." Hooper pulled a folded newspaper from his rear pocket and handed it to Sutton who took it, began to unfold it, and glanced questioningly at Hooper.

"Inside," Hooper said. "Page three."

Sutton opened the paper. He began to read what was printed beneath his picture.

"You're a celebrity of sorts, Luke," Hooper commented when Sutton had finished reading and looked up at him. "Not just here but up in Virginia City too by the looks of things."

Sutton noticed that he had not been reading a local paper. He held in his hands, he noticed for the first time, a copy of Virginia City's *Territorial Enterprise*.

Hooper said, "As winner of that shooting contest we had

ourselves last week, Luke, maybe you'd best start watching your step."

"What do you mean, Cal?"

"Well, some gunfighter or other's liable to come round to see which one of you can shoot faster. There's always jaspers who just can't abide the thought that another man might be faster on the draw than they happen to be and now that you've gotten more than local notoriety—well, I'm sure you take my meaning."

"That contest I won," Sutton said, "was for shooting at targets, not men. It was a marksmanship trial. I'm no gunfighter."

"Some hothead just might try to test the truth of that last statement of yours."

Sutton grinned. "If one does, well, I'll just throw up my hands and beg the man for mercy."

Hooper laughed and then, sobering, said, "I've never met a man I figured to be less likely to do a thing like that when the chips are down than you, Luke."

Sutton made no response. He merely took the iron gate Clay was dragging across the smithy and began to examine it. Then he added more fuel to the fire in the forge, avoiding any green coal, and carefully banked it with wet coal.

When the fire reached a good white heat, he began to heat the bent and twisted metal, hammering it into shape, sparks flying as he worked, sweat slicking his face and dropping from it to hiss in the open flames.

That night at the Grange Hall Sutton stood at the long table that was covered with a white cloth and asked Eileen, who was standing beside him, if she was hungry.

"I am," she admitted, "but those sandwiches look big enough to choke a horse. Sure, and I couldn't finish one all by myself."

Sutton picked up a ham sandwich, broke it in two, and

handed half of it to Eileen. As the two of them ate, a man on a raised platform at the far end of the hall began to sing.

Sam Bass was born in Indiana; it was his native home,
And at the age of seventeen young Sam began to roam.
He started out to Texas, a cowboy for to be,
And a kinder-hearted fellow you scarcely ever'd see.

"Have some of that," Sutton said to Eileen, pointing to the bowl that was heaped high with stewed fruit.

She shook her head. "I couldn't be eating another bite after this." She finished the last of her half of their shared sandwich.

Sutton picked up a cut glass dish, spooned it full of fruit, and began to eat. "Apricots," he said. "Real good. You sure you don't want some, Eileen? They're real tasty."

"No, thank you." She turned around. "Would you be liking some coffee, Luke?"

"I would."

She left him and crossed the room to the potbellied stove on which the coffeepot sat. After pouring two cups of coffee she carried them back and handed one to Sutton.

"Thanks," he said as he took the cup. "It's just the way I like it. Black as the pit of hell and just as hot."

The singer on the platform finished his rendition of "Sam Bass" and, acceding to the shouted requests from the crowd, launched into "The Dying Cowboy."

"Oh, bury me out on the lone prairie,"
The words came low and mournfully,
From the cold, pale lips of a youth who lay
On his dying couch at the close of day.

"Such a sad song," Eileen observed. "I thought this was supposed to be a festive occasion."

"The festivities'll be starting any minute now," Sutton told her. "Look there. The fiddler's all set."

When the singer had concluded his mournful song, he

stepped down from the platform and was immediately replaced by an old man carrying a fiddle and bow.

The old man was joined on the platform by a younger man who raised both of his hands and called out, "Choose your partners!"

A sudden flurry of activity filled the hall as men boldly or shyly approached the women of their choice, their spurs clinking and their eyes sparkling.

"Honor your partners!" the young man called out as the dancers got themselves into position. "Rights the same. Balance you all. Eight hands up . . ."

Sutton and Eileen, in the middle of the floor, raised their arms. They were facing each other, separated by another man and a woman, neither of whom they knew.

". . . *and circle to the left. Brake and run away eight!*"

The square dance began. Eileen's skirt swirled. Sutton's boots thudded on the wooden floor.

"*First couple balance and swing; Promenade the inside ring . . .*"

The square dance proceeded, following the instructions of the caller as the fiddler filled the hall with music.

"*Gents chase and put on style.*
Rehash and a little more style.
Little more style, gents, a little more style."

Sutton, catching Eileen's eye, swiveled his hips.

Eileen smiled and, after weaving in and out with the others in the set, she passed Sutton and whispered, "*Wicked!*"

"*First lady out to the right.*"

Eileen danced to the right.

"*Swing the man that stole the sheep,*" cried the caller and Eileen seized Sutton's hand and swung him as Sutton said, just loud enough for her to hear, an exaggerated expression of anxiety on his face, "I never stole no sheep, ma'am, and that's the plain truth!"

"*Now the one that hauled it home,*

Now the one that eat the meat,
And now the one that gnawed the bone."
The caller caught his breath before continuing with:
"First gent, swing your opposite partner,
Then your turtle dove . . ."
Sutton spun Eileen around.
"Again your opposite partner . . ."
Sutton did the same for the other woman in the set.
"And now your own true love."
He was back with Eileen again.
"Birdie hop out . . ."
Eileen hopped out.
". . . and crow hop in."
Sutton hopped in.
"Yellowhammer right and jaybird left.
Meet your partner and all chew hay,
You know where and I don't care.
Seat your partner in the old armchair."
Sutton seized Eileen's waist, lifted her high above his head, and then plopped her into the nearest chair where she sat laughing and fanning her face with one hand as the fiddler stopped playing and the caller quieted.

One of the dancers called out a request.

The fiddler went to work at once, drawing his bow over the strings of his fiddle, and the caller again ordered everyone to choose their partners.

Sutton held out his hands to Eileen who gasped and said, "For the sake of the dear Saint Patrick, Luke, do let me draw my breath."

He ignored her protest and pulled her to her feet. A moment later, they were dancing again, the fiddle filling the hall with rhythmic music, the voice of the caller loud in the room as he vigorously beat time with one foot.

"First lady out to the right,
Swing Daddy Lannigan,

Then Mother Flannigan,
Now the old man again,
Swing partner around."

By midnight, Eileen insisted she couldn't eat another bite nor did she want another cup of coffee. "Sure, now, and I've downed so many I might sink to the floor and drown at any moment."

Nor did she want to dance, accusing Sutton of having worn her out so that, "I'll have no strength for another square dance before Christmas comes—if then."

They walked home arm in arm, saying little.

Sutton was happy, almost able to forget the pain that lived deep within him beside the lust for vengeance which, on sleepless nights and even in the midst of a crowd, sometimes shouted the hated name so that he could hear nothing else. Now, as he thought of Adam Foss, he gritted his teeth and tightened his hold on Eileen's arm.

"Is something wrong?" she asked him.

"Nope. How could there be on a nice spring night like this one? Look up there at the sky. It's got more stars in it than Abilene's got cows."

When they reached Mrs. Reardon's boardinghouse, Sutton, without saying a word, took Eileen in his arms and kissed her.

She showed no surprise. Her arms went around him and she gripped his shoulders, returning his kiss.

Some moments later, as they separated, she said, "It's late. I should— Luke, what's the matter?"

"Nothing."

"Oh, but there is something," she insisted. "The way you took me before—almost ferociously as if you thought, heaven forbid, that I was about to run away from you."

"I didn't think that."

She stood on tiptoe and kissed him on the lips. "Were I ever to do such a foolish thing, I do fancy you're a fast runner. You could catch me."

"You'd better go in. Like you said, it's late and Mrs. Reardon's boarders, me among them, will be stampeding into the kitchen at first light. They won't want to find you there all red-eyed and weary as a result of this night's debauchery."

"Go on with you! Debauchery indeed!"

"I saw the eyes you were making at every man who laid hands on you when we were dancing."

"You're jealous, I hope?"

"I most certainly am."

"Oh, I'm that glad!" Eileen declared happily, clapping her hands. "Aren't you coming in?"

"Not yet. I want to stay out here for a spell. I'll not be long."

"Good night, Luke."

"Sleep well."

Then she was gone and Sutton stood alone in the quiet night. He went up on the porch and sat down in the swing that was suspended by two lengths of chain from the porch roof. He braced his back against one of the swing's armrests, his boots against the other.

He knew it was good, the way he had been living his life for the past several months. For the first time in years, he had settled down in one place and allowed himself to form firm human relationships with such men as Cal Hooper and with such women as Mrs. Reardon. And with, most especially, Eileen Dugan.

Her image appeared in his mind's eye, smiling at him, beckoning to him. Did he love her? He squeezed his eyes shut, banishing her. He also banished the question he had asked himself instead of answering it. The answer, he knew, would bind him. To her. And to this place—at least for a time before they might decide together to move on.

But he was a man who would not—dare not—let himself be bound by anyone or anything. Not now. Not yet.

Silently, he cursed the four men who had changed his life

and made it less than his own. The four men who had forced him to leave his homeplace and wander rootless as a tumble-weed ever since, in search of them.

He could stop his hunting. End it.

"*No!*" he said aloud, his voice harsh and angry.

His anger stiffened his body and he thrust out a boot and pushed against the floor of the porch. The swing, creaking, moved backward.

At the same instant, the quiet of the night was shattered as a rifle report sounded and the shell slammed into the wall behind the spot where Sutton had been sitting only a moment ago.

As the swing began to retrace its arc, he threw himself from it and hit the floor.

A second shot rang out.

He heard the bullet bury itself in the wooden wall behind him.

Then he was up and bounding effortlessly over the porch railing. He went zigzagging across the lawn and then across the street in the direction from which the two shots had come.

CHAPTER 2

When he reached the opposite side of the street, Sutton crouched low and ran along beside the white picket fence that enclosed the house opposite Mrs. Reardon's.

His heart was hammering, not so much from his exertions as from the excitement that was surging within him.

He had seen the two bursts of flame from the rifle so he

knew that whoever had tried to kill him had fired from beside the house just beyond the picket fence. He halted and peered through the pickets. He saw only shadows created by the half-moon in the sky above him. He heard only silence.

Automatically, his right hand went to his hip. But his six-gun was in his bedroom as was his cartridge belt.

Fool, he thought. I'm a fool for chasing after a rifleman, with no weapon to defend myself should he decide to try again to take me.

When the shots had ripped through the night, he had reacted almost without thought. Someone was trying to kill him. He'd get that someone. Kill him? He didn't know.

A question rattled around in his mind: Who was trying to kill him?

Another question: Why was the unknown someone trying to kill him?

There was no mistaking the gunman's intent. Sutton had been alone on the porch. There was no one else abroad in the night. Someone had stalked him.

He saw lamplight spill from inside the house he was watching. Someone inside, he supposed, had heard the shots. Or had the person who fired them gone inside?

He heard the sound of someone running.

Which way?

He listened carefully. The footsteps began to fade. He sprang erect and, as he vaulted the picket fence, he heard a wooden gate clack shut behind the house. He headed for it and went through it on the run.

Someone—one more shadow in the night—was running down the alley that separated the houses from the commercial warehouses behind them. Whoever it was had a rifle. Sutton suddenly turned into the darkness between two warehouses.

When he reached the outside staircase that led to the second floor of the warehouse on his left, he took the stairs two at a time. At the second-floor landing, he leaped up and

seized the edge of the roof. He hauled himself up and over
the edge, his boots scraping the side of the building, until he
lay belly down on the roof. He was up in an instant and running across the flat roof. When he reached its end, he leaped
across the space that separated the warehouse he was on from
the building next door and then, a moment after landing on
the neighboring roof, he turned and ran to the front of the
building.

He'd been right.

Because the alley behind the warehouses curved, the man
he was pursuing had been forced to follow it and now Sutton
saw him emerging just below him.

Sutton crouched and then leaped down onto the overhang
below him. The moment he landed, he leaped again and
landed on the fleeing figure below him.

He brought the man down to the ground. They rolled over.
Sutton tore the rifle from the man's hand and, as he did so,
the man kneed him in the groin.

Sutton gasped and dropped the rifle.

The man he was straddling kneed him again, causing Sutton to double over in pain.

The man sprang to his feet and kicked out at Sutton.

But Sutton threw himself to one side, hitting the ground
hard and rolling over.

As the man lunged for his rifle, Sutton got to his knees. He
sprang forward and sprawled face down in the dirt. But the
fingers of his right hand closed on the rifle barrel. As its
owner tried to wrest it from him, Sutton got to his knees and
swung the rifle. The stock caught his assailant in the ribs and
Sutton heard bone crack.

The man let out a yelp and ran.

Sutton got up and went after him.

They raced down the street through the flood of shadows.
Sutton, gaining on the man, made a choice. He dropped the
rifle and threw himself forward.

His arms went around the fleeing man's legs, dropping him. He turned him over, drove a fist into the man's face, and then another.

The man reached up and seized Sutton's shirt with both hands. Sutton tore them free, ripping his shirt in the process. The man tried to bring his knee up. Sutton sat down heavily on his prisoner's thighs, thereby preventing the maneuver. He seized the man's wrists and pinned them to the ground. Bending over close to the man's face, he asked, "Who are you?"

The man turned his head to one side as if to avoid the question.

"Why'd you try it?"

The man was silent.

Sutton got to his feet, hauling the man up with him, and slammed him up against the wall of the warehouse. He drew him close and then turned him around. He grabbed a fistful of the man's pants, another fistful of his shirt, and flung him head first against the wall.

The man screamed as he struck the wall. He slumped to the ground.

Sutton hauled him up again, turned him around, and drew back his left fist.

"No!" the man muttered.

Sutton's fist landed on his jaw. He heard one or more of the man's teeth snap. His fist came away bloody.

"Tell me!" he commanded.

". . . hired me."

"Who hired you to kill me?"

The man suddenly threw himself to one side, breaking free of Sutton. He ran up the alley, his arms flailing wildly.

Sutton went after him a second time. He caught him, spun him around, hooked a toe of his right boot behind the man's knee, jerked his leg forward, and the man fell on his back.

He tried to rise but Sutton stepped forward until his boots were planted on both sides of the man's thighs. "You move,

I'll stomp you so's you'll never be a daddy again if you are one now. You move again and I'll stomp you so hard your supper'll be on the ground for folks from all over to take a look at."

The man blubbered and wiped his bloody mouth with the back of one hairy hand. "Let me go," he muttered. "I won't ever do it again. Mister, I promise you as the Lord's my witness you'll never see me again."

"Maybe your promise is good enough for the Lord. It's not good enough for me. Now, who hired you to kill me?"

Sutton thought the man sprawled at his feet had sighed.

"Foss."

Sutton's body tensed. His mind raced. "Adam Foss?"

The man nodded. Moonlight made the blood on his lips and stubbled chin glisten.

"Adam Foss," Sutton repeated softly, the tension slowly draining away. He felt a keen joy well up within him. He felt almost friendly toward the man lying before him. "I know why Foss hired you. What I don't know is where he is. I want to know where he is. You're going to tell me."

"Virginia City."

"Foss is in Virginia City." It was a statement, not a question. "Where exactly in Virginia City?"

The man suddenly seized Sutton's boots and jerked him off his feet. Sutton hit the ground as the man scrambled up and raced away from him.

Sutton got up fast and began to run.

A shot rang out.

The man Sutton was pursuing staggered. He took several more steps, slowing, and then he fell.

A bulky man stepped out of the shadows. As Sutton came abreast of him, the man said, "Don't move, mister, or you're next."

Sutton halted. His arms rose. He swore.

The gunman on the ground was dead. Sutton had no doubt

about it. His assailant had been blown nearly in half at close range by the shotgun the bulky man was now holding on him.

"Don't I know you?" asked the man with the shotgun, squinting at Sutton.

"You might have seen me about town. I live at Mrs. Reardon's boardinghouse. Work for Mr. Hooper at the smithy."

"The smithy. That's where I seen you. What are you doing out here in the middle of the night shooting things up?"

Sutton explained.

"So that's what happened, is it," the man commented when Sutton had finished. "When I heard the shooting and then all the commotion out here, I figured I'd better get busy and protect my wife and family. Glad to have been able to do you a good turn."

"I wish you hadn't done it," Sutton said. He turned on his heels and walked away from the man with the shotgun who stood staring after him, scratching his head in bewilderment.

He didn't answer my question, Sutton thought as he made his way back to Mrs. Reardon's boardinghouse. I don't know where to find Foss in Virginia City. But he didn't let that fact discourage him. As he made his way between the two warehouses, he decided that it wouldn't be all that hard to find Foss in Virginia City. He'd go there. He'd ask around. It might turn out to be easy to track Foss down. Once he did . . .

How, he began to wonder as he walked, had Foss known where to find him—where to send the hired gun after him? The answer came to him in a flash. The shooting contest last week. More precisely, the picture of himself that had been printed in Virginia City's *Territorial Enterprise,* the one Cal Hooper had shown him earlier in the day.

You made a mistake, Foss, he thought as he picked up the rifle that he had dropped earlier. You should have sent a better man after me.

He came around the side of the house with the picket fence and, across the street, he saw Eileen standing on the lawn, wearing a white flannel nightgown and a ruffled white night-cap. When she saw him, she let out a brief cry and then she was running across the street and into his arms.

"Luke, I was so worried! What a fright you gave me! I heard shooting and I came downstairs and you weren't any-where to be seen. *Luke!*" She held him tightly.

He soothed her, murmuring meaningless words because ev-erything was not alright now, was not over—not for him. It was all wrong and it was beginning again, this time with the man—the murderer—Adam Foss.

"What happened, Luke? What in the world happened?"

"There was a man. He shot at me. Twice." Sutton's voice was low, his expression grim as he stood with his arm around Eileen staring into the darkness and seeing only the face of Adam Foss.

"Why?"

Sutton wanted to shout the answer to her question, make the night know it—the whole world. "It's a matter between me and him," was all he said.

Eileen drew back and looked into his eyes. Anxiety was etched on her features. Her eyes, still wide with alarm, searched his.

"We'll go inside," Sutton told her.

With their arms around one another's waists, they did.

"Could you drink a nice hot cup of tea, Luke?" Eileen tried a smile that was a wan imitation of her usually dazzling one. "I've not yet met an Irishman who would not welcome a cup of tea whether it be offered him at a wedding or a wake."

Sutton wanted something stronger. "Tea'll be just fine. Have a cup with me."

They went into the kitchen and he placed the rifle on the table as Eileen put the kettle on. "I was that worried," she said as she fired up the stove. "Go after him, do, I told myself when I came out and found you gone. But I was too fright-ened to so much as move an eyebrow, don't you know?"

As she proceeded to describe how Mrs. Reardon and some

of the boarders had come downstairs with her before she persuaded them to return to bed, Sutton sat at the table, his
fingers tightly intertwined.

When she had poured tea for both of them and placed the
cozy over the china pot, she sat down next to him and took
his hand. "It's glad I am, Luke, that you're alright. But the
other man—what happened to him?"

"Dead."

"Dead," she repeated, her tone hollow. Then, "You killed
him."

Sutton shook his head. "A man came out of nowhere. With
a shotgun. He was the one killed him."

"I'll find that darling man first thing in the morning and
give him a great big kiss for saving your life."

"Eileen—"

She put down the cup she had been about to drink from.
"Luke?"

He drew a deep breath. "I have to—in the morning—
there's someone in Virginia City I have to see."

Eileen visibly relaxed. "You sound so somber about taking
such a short trip."

"It's not that."

"Then what's brought the storm clouds to your brow?"

"I don't know how long I'll be there. I don't know if I'll
have to go on from there."

Eileen looked down at her cup. Her hands reached out to
encircle it as if seeking warmth from it. Steam rose from it
and she seemed to be watching it swirl about before it disappeared.

"Will you do something for me in the morning, Eileen?"

"What?"

"Go tell Cal Hooper I won't be coming in to the smithy.
Tell him I had to go to Virginia City."

"I'll tell him." Eileen turned and stared at Sutton. "When
shall I tell Mr. Hooper you'll be back?"

"Tell him I don't know."

"Luke, don't go to Virginia City."

He glanced at her.

"Something's wrong. I can feel it. I'm afraid to ask you what it is. It's so afraid I am to hear what you might tell me. Luke, please don't go."

"I've got to go."

"But you will come back—someday."

"I have to be honest with you, Eileen. I don't know if I ever will."

"Because the man you're going to find might kill you. It's true, isn't it? Just as that man tried to kill you tonight."

"It's true."

"Luke, what about me? What about you and me? I thought—" She dropped her eyes. "I thought you cared about me. A little maybe."

He warned himself not to touch her. It would make matters harder. "I do care about you, Eileen. All I can tell you— and I know it doesn't help what you're feeling—is that I've got to go."

She sprang to her feet, knocking over her chair in the process. "I loved you, Luke! I thought you might someday love me!" She fled from the room, her hands covering her face.

Her sobs, as she ran up the stairs to the second floor, drifted back to Sutton who still sat at the table, his hands now forming fists as he silently damned Adam Foss and the hold the man had on him which had prevented him for three years from living his own life, free of ghosts from the deadly past.

Sutton stood alone the next morning, his carpetbag resting beside his boots, on the platform of the depot as he waited for the train to arrive.

He had risen before dawn and, by the light of a lamp in the kitchen, had penciled a brief note to Mrs. Reardon explaining that he was leaving for Virginia City and thanking her for all she had done for him during his stay at her boardinghouse.

He had not seen Eileen before leaving and now, glancing over his shoulder from time to time, he wondered if she would appear to bid him good-bye. He wished she would. He hoped she wouldn't. He wanted to see her but he knew that another meeting would probably only awaken the pain both of them had experienced the night before. Still, his attention was attracted by every woman he saw in the distance. But none of them was Eileen.

As the train, some twenty minutes later, pulled into the station with a shriek of its whistle and the grinding of its wheels against the rails, Sutton did not immediately board it. He walked, carpetbag in hand, back and forth along the platform, past the four freight cars and the two passenger cars, watching passengers disembark and other passengers board the train, still searching for Eileen without admitting the fact to himself.

"All *aboard!*"

After taking one last glance around him, Sutton jumped up on the platform of the first passenger car. He went through the door which had a frosted glass pane set in it and dropped down into an empty seat beside a man with a tawny mustache, round face, and bright blue eyes. He placed his carpetbag under the seat and settled himself for the twenty-one-mile journey to Virginia City.

"Going to Virginia City, are thee, my son?"

Sutton glanced at the man sitting next to the window who was smiling at him. No older than me, he thought. So what's this "my son" business? He nodded.

"To dig for some silver?"

"Nope."

"Then it's business thee 'as waiting for thee there."

"Maybe."

"Are thee in the way of knowing anybody in the city?"

"I might."

"My older brother, a fine lad Richie is, 'e's there along with all that silver just crying out to be found. 'E came over a year ago and headed straight for California. But where 'e wound up, ah, that's another story. He sent me a letter 'e did and told me to come and 'ere I am and full of the fidgets. If we don't get there soon, I'm likely to bust apart, 'tis that excited I am to be on my way."

Sutton had noticed the man's accent when he had first spoken. "You're out from England?"

"I am. Cornwall is what I left behind me. Along with two sisters and my widowed mother, all of them praying that Richie and me will strike it rich in America and ease the rest of their way in the world."

Sutton leaned back, slid down in the seat, and pulled his hat down over his face. He folded his arms across his chest and crossed his booted ankles.

Silence prevailed. But only for a moment.

"My name's Jack Penrose."

Sutton pushed his hat up on his forehead. He shook Penrose's outstretched hand and the man's smile broadened.

"Thee are an American?" Penrose asked.

Sutton nodded, refolding his arms.

"What part?"

"All of me."

Penrose laughed, an airy, somewhat boyish, sound.

"I meant to say what part of America are thee from?"

"Texas."

"A cowboy!" Penrose exclaimed. "I've never met my first one till now. Do people call thee Tex?"

"Name's Sutton. Luke Sutton."

"I'm glad to know thee, Luke, my son. I am all of that."

Sutton was aware of the fact that his bitterness which had resulted from his abrupt departure from Carson City and the friends he had made—particularly Eileen Dugan—was showing, although Penrose didn't seem to be aware of it or, if he were, it apparently didn't bother the man.

He looked out the window as the train wound its way through the rocky gorge that had been blasted in the hills to lay the crooked route the train was following over trestles and through dark tunnels. As the train continued its gradual ascent, he pulled his hat down over his face again.

Penrose said, "'Ow long will it be taking us, this trip, do thee 'appen to know?"

Sutton gave up. He sat up, tilted his hat back on his head, and said, "Not all that long. Simmer down and enjoy the ride, Jack."

"Are thee 'ungry, Luke?"

Sutton, having had no breakfast, was but he shook his head as Penrose began to unwrap the butcher paper covering a parcel that was resting in his lap.

As if he hadn't seen Sutton shake his head, Penrose handed him a roast beef sandwich. "I bought these sandwiches a while back and I see that I 'ave gone and bought more than my stomach will accommodate. 'Ere, take this one, Luke, and thee'll be 'elping me escape the sin of waste."

Sutton, meeting Penrose's gaze and seeing his almost ingenuous smile that seemed to light up the car, took the sandwich and bit into it.

"Ah now, aren't these good?" Penrose exclaimed as he ate heartily.

Sutton smiled. It was impossible not to like Penrose. He was cheerful, hopeful, and even willing, Sutton thought, to put up with somebody as cranky as I've been being with him.

Penrose was on his feet the instant he caught his first glimpse of Virginia City through the train window. "There she is, Luke. Will thee take a look at 'er now? She's a veritable metropolis." He seized his leather satchel from beneath his seat and climbed over Sutton. "Come along, my son, 'tis 'ere we are and 'tis time we were getting off this train and out into the wild western air again."

Luke, smiling to himself, retrieved his carpetbag and walked down the aisle. He went through the door and then stepped down from the platform.

A hand clapped him on the back and he spun around.

"Luke, come along now, my son," Penrose declared. "I'll be introducing thee to my brother, Richie. Oh, thee will take a fancy to 'im I've no doubt about that. Richie can sing as good as any Welshman and better than any Irishman, even one that is sober."

Sutton stared up at the still snow-packed peaks of the Sierras. He put up a hand to hold his hat which was threatening to blow away because of the strong wind that swooped down over the city from the towering mountains.

He coughed and looked up at the almost tangible clouds of swirling smoke and alkali from which was sifting a fine dry dust. A moment later, the dust was in his mouth and he spat to rid himself of it—fruitlessly.

He stared up a wide dirt street that was bordered on both sides by an unbroken line of sawmills, quartz mills, tunnels, dumps, sluices, waterwheels, frame shanties, wooden houses, and adobes.

"I say, sorr," Penrose was saying to a man who had been passing by. "Where would I find—one moment, sorr." He pulled a crumpled piece of paper from his pocket. "C Street," he said.

"You're looking at it, mister."

"Ah, 'tis that street there, is it?" Penrose said, pointing to the one Sutton had been studying.

When the man had gone, Penrose hooked his arm in Sutton's. "Walk along with me, Luke. Richie built himself a little house on C Street and 'tis C Street we're on."

"Jack, I think I'd best—"

But Penrose was paying no attention to Sutton's mild protest. Instead, he was dragging him along the street which sloped upward at a steep angle.

"Look out!" Sutton said and pulled Penrose back as a heavily laden ore wagon drawn by four mules rumbled past them, almost running them both down.

"Look there, Luke!" Penrose cried excitedly and Sutton looked in the direction his companion had pointed to see several imposing six-story brick buildings sporting wide balconies. French windows opened off the second stories of each of the buildings.

"Those must be the 'omes of the gentry," Penrose commented, nodding to himself. "Or maybe 'tis common folk like thee and me who've struck it rich and can amble about in their 'alls and arcades."

Sutton smiled at the irrepressible note of hope he heard in Penrose's voice.

As they proceeded to climb C Street, they became immersed in a throng that seemed to have erupted from nowhere. Miners, grime blackening their faces, streamed past them, talking loudly, occasionally laughing, coughing often. Chinese fruit vendors trotted about conversing shrilly with one another, their fruit baskets suspended from both ends of the poles they balanced on their thin shoulders. Paiutes argued vociferously. Women herded chattering children through the deepening dusk. An organ grinder turned the crank of his organ and his monkey, which wore a faded red fez, scampered at the end of its long chain and held out its cup for coins. A lamplighter sang as he made his rounds, illuminating the gas jets that were perched atop iron standards.

To Sutton the place sounded like Bedlam.

Newsboys were selling—at the top of their voices—the latest edition of the *Territorial Enterprise*. Raucous music drifted through the open doors of hurdy-gurdy joints. There was the sharp sound of whips cracking over the heads of the mules that were hauling the countless ore wagons which were clogging the street. The muted sounds of distant explosions in the mines followed one after another, seemingly without pause.

"There 'tis!" Penrose shouted happily above the din and then he proceeded to drag Sutton toward the squat shanty that nestled among others of its kind.

"How do you know—" And then Sutton knew how Penrose had recognized his brother's home. The name Penrose was neatly lettered in white paint on the front door.

"Richie, my 'andsome!" Penrose shouted and, releasing his hold on Sutton's arm, raced toward the closed door. When he reached it, he tried to open it and, finding it locked, began to pound on it, shouting his brother's name at the top of his voice.

"Maybe he's not home," Sutton volunteered after joining Penrose at the door.

"Perhaps 'e isn't," Penrose said, undaunted by his failure to raise a response from inside the house. "We'll have to content ourselves with waiting for 'im to come 'ome."

"You wait for him, Jack. I've got to find me some lodgings for the night."

" 'Ere, now, old son, don't go running off on me. Wait a bit till Richie gets back. We'll 'ave a fine time, the three of us, thee'll see."

"Jack, I—"

A young woman came out of the house next door and stood staring at Sutton and Penrose, her face grim.

Sutton bowed slightly and touched the brim of his hat to her.

"Is it Richard Penrose you're after?" she asked.

"Ah, 'tis that, my beauty," Penrose declared with animation. "Now, can thee tell me where to find my brother?"

Sutton thought the woman's face had darkened at the sound of the word "brother" but he wasn't sure. It might have

only seemed to have done so because of the smoke still swirling in the air.

"He's been gone these past two months, Richard has," the
woman said somberly.

Penrose's face fell. His smile evaporated. "Richie's gone?
Where?"

"It was the miner's consumption that took him off, damn it
to hell. Doesn't my own husband have a touch of it now? He's
coughing his lungs out just like poor Richard did there at the
end and it's a sorry thing to have to hear, I can tell you, what
with me saddled with three that are little more than babes."

"Dead?" Penrose's word hung in the air, thicker than the
smoke.

"We, some of us, buried him up on Mount Davidson," the
woman said. "It's a shame it is that you've come to find him
long gone." The woman turned, about to re-enter her house.
"It's sorry I am for your trouble, Mr. Penrose." Then she
was gone.

Penrose looked mournfully at Sutton. His leather satchel
fell from his hand.

"I'm real sorry," Sutton said softly. "It's hard to lose a
brother."

"Harder when you loved 'im so the way I loved Richie,"
Penrose murmured. "Since we were little 'uns we got along,
Richie and me did. There was fighting, sure. But there was
fun as well. We were chums, Richie and me."

The woman reappeared. She walked wearily up to Penrose
and handed him something.

Penrose looked down at the key in his hand.

"To Richard's house," she said. "He asked us before he was
took to give it to you if you ever came out from England. He
said he thought you'd come. If you did, he said, he wanted
you to have his house."

"I thank thee," Penrose said, staring at the iron key in his
hand.

When the woman had gone, Sutton took the key from Penrose's hand and unlocked the door. He took Penrose by the arm, led him inside the shanty, and then sat him down in a wooden chair in the sparsely furnished room.

A moment later, after bringing in Penrose's satchel, he said, "I'll come by tomorrow or the next day, Jack, to see how you're doing."

"Thee needs a place to stay, Luke. This place would do thee well enough, wouldn't it?"

"I thought—a boardinghouse might be—"

"I've not the least right," Penrose said. "But were thee to see thy way clear to spend the night 'ere with me, we could talk. I could tell thee all about Richie and how we got along so fine, the two of us."

Sutton had trouble meeting Penrose's suddenly dull eyes. He noticed his slack features. "I thank you kindly for letting me stay the night, Jack. I'd like to hear about you and your brother. What was Richie like?"

Penrose tried to smile and then he began to tell Sutton about his brother.

As the night deepened outside the shanty, Sutton heard the love hidden behind Penrose's words. He remembered Dan, and fully understood why Penrose had tears streaming down his cheeks as he talked of his brother who was lost to him for good.

CHAPTER 3

The following morning, Sutton and Penrose made their way in silence down the sloping side of Mount Davidson.

The wind was at their backs, strong as usual, seeming to be hurrying them along toward Virginia City sprawled below them. Sutton made out many of the landmarks of the city as he walked slightly behind Penrose, the wind whipping his hair and threatening at any moment to lift his hat and send it spinning down onto one of the roofs below.

Piper's Opera House gleamed whitely in the sunlight beneath its dark roof and the Fourth Ward School stood tall and seemingly aloof at the end of C Street. He saw the five-story brick building with its windows framed by white marble arches that was the famed International Hotel.

"I looked everywhere," Penrose said, breaking their silence. "But I could find myself not a one."

"Not a one of what?"

"Flowers. Nothing but slag heaps and dust everywhere. Men have rid this land of its beauty in their search for silver. There's not a flower to be found. Only monuments to man's great greed." Penrose flung out a hand and swept it in front of him to encompass the ore mills, timber tramways, ore car trestles, and hoisting works that covered the face of the land.

"There's a saying," Sutton mused, "that I've heard a time or two. 'Take what you want,' God said. 'And pay for it.'"

"Ah, Luke, my son, men have taken 'ere." Penrose again swung his arm in a gesture that was faintly contemptuous, slightly aggressive. "And will you look now at the terrible price they've paid for it? Not a flower to be found to lay on poor Richie's grave. Hardly a tree to be seen, all of them cut down to shore up the tunnels beneath our feet. 'Tis a shame, it is."

"It's progress, a man might say."

Penrose snorted. "In the old country, there were flowers everywhere. Grass. The banks of the river Tamar would be blooming all spring and summer long both on the Cornwall and the Devonshire sides with more kinds of posies than thee could count were thee to use not only thy fingers but all ten of thy toes as well."

"You told me last night that there were mines in Cornwall too," Sutton reminded him.

"Ah, and so there were. Ugly things like what thee sees

about thee 'ere. We mined copper, iron, granite, slate, and serpentine. We—" Penrose slowed his pace until Sutton was walking beside him. "I see what thee are driving at, now, don't I, Luke?"

"Things are pretty much the same everywhere a man goes. So are people. You make the best of things. Try to."

Penrose sneezed. He blew his nose, using two fingers and the wind that was riding down the mountain. "Damn this alkali dust!" he sputtered. "Well, perhaps it will be not as nasty down in the mines, though I've little hope on that score."

"You're planning on going down in the mines to work?"

"Thee said thyself, Luke, that things are much the same everywhere. I came from the mines in Cornwall to the mines 'ere. Now, what else would I do? What else am I fit to do?"

"Men die in the mines."

"They do that, I'll grant thee. But don't they die out in the sun too beneath the bright blue sky with their eyes on white sheep grazing high up on green hillsides?"

Penrose was silent a moment and Sutton wondered if he was remembering Richie. Then he spoke, his quizzical eyes on Sutton. "What do thee 'ave it in mind to do, my son?"

What indeed, Sutton wondered. And thought, find Foss. He answered, "I'm rapidly running out of cash money and that's a fact. I'll have to find me something to help hold body and soul together until—" He looked away, leaving his statement unfinished.

Penrose pointed.

Sutton looked at the sign Penrose had pointed out.

High Stakes Mine, it said. It hung on the hoisting works which stood in the midst of a cluster of unpainted wooden buildings.

"The office, 'tis over there, Luke. Come along with me. Maybe we can find ourselves something to do that will keep us both out of mischief."

As Penrose headed for the office, Sutton followed him, reluctant to apply for a job as a miner but keenly aware of the fact that he had little money left in his pocket and that it would not last him very long in an expensive place like Virginia City.

He entered the office behind Penrose and heard his companion say to the lean man who was seated behind a desk, "I'd like to see the mine superintendent."

"I'm him."

"I've come to go to work for thee, sorr. My name's Penrose."

Sutton smiled to himself at Penrose's jaunty self-confidence, his buoyant optimism. He sounded as if he were doing the mine superintendent a favor.

"You're a Britisher?" the superintendent asked.

"From Cornwall, sorr," Penrose answered. "A miner I've been since I was thirteen." He held out his hands, palms up and, as the man behind the desk looked at them, he said, "My references, sorr."

Sutton caught a glimpse of Penrose's callused hands as the superintendent said, "You Cousin Jacks generally do good hard work, so we've found."

"Cousin Jacks?" Penrose cocked his head to one side, puzzled.

The superintendent smiled. "When we ask one of you men from Cornwall if you have a relative at home who would consider coming over here to work in the mines, it's more than likely that the answer will be, 'Well, sorr, I have a Cousin Jack who might.'"

Penrose smiled broadly.

"We're not hiring," the superintendent told him bluntly.

Penrose's face fell.

"But I'll make an exception in your case. We can't have too many Cornishmen working for us. Each one of you's worth two of any other kind of laborer."

Penrose beamed.

"When can you start?"

"Why, right this very minute, sorr, if that's to thy pleasure."
He hesitated and then, "Thee will want to be hiring my friend
'ere, now won't thee, sorr? Look at those shoulders of 'is and
that strong back. 'E's got good wind, 'e 'as."

The superintendent shook his head. "I shouldn't be taking
you on. I'm certainly not taking on anybody else."

Penrose glanced at Sutton and Sutton shrugged.

"I come to thee as part of a pair, sorr," Penrose said po-
litely. "Thee takes me, thee takes 'im too."

The superintendent glared at Penrose. Picking up a pencil,
he pointed it at Penrose and said, "If you want to work here
at the High Stakes, you can. *You* can," he repeated, his impli-
cation clear.

"Jack," Sutton said softly. "It's alright. Take the job. I'll find
something."

"I do sorely need it, this job," Penrose said as softly, "but—"

"Take it. I'll see you at home tonight."

Sutton turned and quickly left the office. He made his way
down the slope to the town and walked through it. Anyone
observing him would have assumed that he was strolling
aimlessly to take in the sights of the surging city that lay scat-
tered below the looming mountain ranges. But he was neither
strolling aimlessly nor was he merely taking in the sights as
any casual visitor to the city might. No man's face escaped his
notice. He paused in the doorways of saloons and looked in,
searching the faces within and not finding the man he was
hunting.

He decided to make inquiries and went into the Wells
Fargo bank and then the express office. He asked his ques-
tion, the one he had asked in countless towns throughout the
West during the past three years. Did anyone know a man by
the name of Adam Foss? Receiving a negative reply, he left.
During the next hour he visited Bricket's recorder's office,
Gardiner's livery, the blacksmith shop of Willard and Eells,

Smith's Pioneer Drug Store, the office of Billet and Ferris, mining claims agents, and Grosetta and Company's Virginia Saloon.

Foss, he had reasoned, might be known in any one of these establishments.

He was not.

Heads shook when Sutton asked his question. Men—and women—told him they had never heard the name Adam Foss.

Sutton, after eating a meal in Folger's Restaurant which filled him without being particularly pleasing, made his way back up C Street toward the shanty beyond which were the sentinel shapes of the mountains. He halted in front of an imposing red-brick, iron-faced building which had a sign above its entrance which read:

Office of the
TERRITORIAL ENTERPRISE

He went through the door which was flanked by two windows and leaned on a shelf-like structure which was just a few feet inside the door. To the woman at the desk who looked up at him, he said, "I'd be obliged if I could talk to the man who runs your newspaper."

"You have business with Mr. Wright?" she inquired. "He's a very busy man. Editing the *Enterprise* leaves him little time for anything else."

"I'd just like to ask him one question. Won't take me longer'n a few seconds to do it."

The woman rose and went to a door behind her. She opened it and called out, "Mr. Wright! There's a man here to see you."

As she returned to her seat, a tall man with black hair as straight as Sutton's came through the door. His cheeks were clean-shaven but he wore a mustache and goatee which met at the corners of his thin lips. He had a broad forehead, big ears, and a large nose. His dark eyes were narrow and bright as he peered at Sutton.

"I'm William Wright," he said in a pleasant voice. But his eyes remained cool.

"Sutton. You can tell me if you've ever heard of a man here in the city name of Adam Foss." Sutton caught the woman's eye. "Told you it wouldn't take long." He grinned at her.

"Foss," Wright repeated. "Adam Foss. No, I don't think so. May I ask whether you have any reason to believe your Mr. Foss is here in Virginia City?"

"I have reason to believe he is, yes."

"May I ask why you are inquiring about the man?"

"It's a personal matter."

"I see. Well, actually I don't see but that's of no consequence."

"I thank you for your time, Mr. Wright."

As Sutton turned to go, Wright asked, "Are you by any chance affiliated with the law, Mr. Sutton?"

"Nope." Not unless you consider that there's a five-hundred-dollar bounty on my head, Sutton thought.

"The military?"

"The military? Me? I've had no connection with them since I scouted for the cavalry some years back. What might you have in mind, Mr. Wright?"

"There are, I've noticed, a number of strangers in town of late. There has been talk among members of the Mine Owners' Association of trouble, and the trouble they are concerned about is the possible threat of strikes by the men in the mines. Rumor has it that strike breakers will be called in if such an event occurs. Possibly even some members of the state militia."

"That's no concern of mine. I'm neither a miner nor a mine owner. Good day, Mr. Wright."

Once outside on C Street again, Sutton made his way to the

shanty he shared with Penrose. As he entered it, he found
Penrose sitting on one of the two cots in the large room, a
handbill in his lap.

"There thee are, my son. Come take a look at this."

Sutton took the handbill Penrose held out to him and read
it. "So there's to be a drilling contest."

"Day after tomorrow," Penrose said, nodding enthusi-
astically. "The winners, that handbill says, of the double-jacking contest will 'ave five 'undred dollars they didn't 'ave before to split between them. Now, doesn't that warm thy heart
and put thy empty pockets to 'oping, Luke?"

"My pockets aren't empty." But uncomfortably close to
being so, he thought wryly.

"Mine are," Penrose said matter-of-factly, turning them out.
"I don't get my first pay for a whole week yet. But I'll make
do somehow till we win the double-jacking contest."

"Until *we* win—"

Penrose leaped to his feet and flung an arm around Sutton's
shoulder. "Did thee ever do any 'ard rock drilling, my son?"

"Some," Sutton answered grimly, remembering the degrad-
ing days he had spent as a slave laborer in a gold mine in the
Dakota Badlands.

"My father, bless him," Penrose declared, "was one of the
best and fastest drillers in the old country, that 'e was now.
Taught me 'ow, though I'm not close to being as good as 'e
was. But I can 'old my own, I can. And with thee as my partner, why, there's no way we can lose."

"I'm not sure—"

"Tomorrow," Penrose said thoughtfully, "when I come up
from working the mine, I'll find a piece of granite, get a
sledge and steel, and I'll teach thee all thee'll need to know so
that the two of us can walk off with the five 'undred dollars
the day after tomorrow."

Sutton was about to speak, to protest, but Penrose interrupted him.

"Now, my son, the trick is in the changing from sledge to steel and then back again. A man must be quick."

Sutton shook his head. He smiled. He thought of the five hundred dollars which, divided in half if he and Jack Penrose won the double-jacking contest, would put two hundred and fifty dollars in his pocket.

"So thee will give it a try with me?" Penrose asked hopefully.

"I will, Jack. I certainly will do that."

Two days later, Sutton and Penrose stood waiting on the platform of the depot as shouts went up from the crowd that had gathered to witness the drilling contest.

Men made feverish bets among themselves on their favorite teams of drillers. The odds were shouted from one knot of eager gamblers to the next.

The sun streamed down, making the day hot, and the women in the crowd unfolded and raised their brightly colored parasols as they stood waiting for the contest to begin.

On a siding stood a flatcar and on the flatcar rested a six-foot-thick block of Gunnison granite of uniform hardness, its upper surface dressed flat. Four solid posts placed at either end of the block of granite supported a flat scaffolding with a square hole cut in its center to allow for drilling.

Cheers went up from the crowd as a heavyset man sporting a half-moon beard climbed the short ladder to the scaffolding and then held up his hands for silence. As the crowd quieted, he beckoned and another man mounted the ladder and joined him on the platform.

The bearded man took an Ingersoll watch from the pocket of his vest and announced, "The drilling contest, ladies and gentlemen, is about to begin." He turned to the man on his right who displayed a yardstick he was holding. "As many of you know," the timekeeper bellowed over the heads of the shifting, restless crowd, "the local drilling record in Washoe is twenty-two and five eighths inches. We have every hope of breaking that record today as a result of the herculean efforts about to be expended by our three valorous teams of drillers."

"Have thee got the drills, old son?" Penrose asked Sutton.

"All ten of them," Sutton answered. "And each one's as sharp as a porcupine's quills."

"I've got mop rags," Penrose said, patting his pocket. Nervously, he pulled on the ends of his mustache with his free hand. In his other hand was the handle of a nine-pound sledge, its hammer resting on the ground. "There goes the first team," he said, his voice hushed.

Sutton watched as two brawny men climbed the ladder and began to make their preparations. One man knelt and placed a hexagon-shaped steel drill against the upper surface of the granite block. The other man, gauging his distance, stepped backward, his eye on the drill in his partner's hands. The man holding the drill looked up. The other man glanced at the timekeeper who raised a hand, peered at his watch, and then brought his hand down while simultaneously shouting, "*Go!*"

Down came the sledge to clang against the head of the drill. The man holding the drill gave it a quarter turn. Down came the hammer again.

Someone in the crowd shouted, "*Two!*"

As the minutes passed, other men in the crowd took up the chant that was recording the number of strokes being made per minute.

"—fifty-*one,* fifty-*two,* fifty-*three*—"

"Water!" shouted the man swinging the sledge and the official standing near him dropped his yardstick and, using a tin cup, scooped water from a barrel and poured it in the hole that was being drilled to cool the steel and settle the loose fragments of granite within it.

Fifteen minutes after the drilling had begun, the timekeeper shouted, "*Stop!*"

The two sweating men stopped. The man holding the drill got to his feet as the official with the yardstick proceeded to measure the depth of the hole the team had drilled.

A moment later, one of them shouted to the crowd. "Nineteen and one quarter inches!"

A cheer went up from the crowd.

Growlers of beer were passed from hand to hand.

Women twirled their parasols in gay tribute to the drilling team's prowess.

"Next team!" cried the timekeeper. "Jack Penrose and Luke Sutton!"

"Are thee ready to win that five-'undred-dollar prize, my son?" Penrose asked, giving Sutton a broad smile.

"I am that, Jack, if the good Lord's willing and the river don't rise."

"Come along then, Luke."

Penrose, the hammer in his hand, made for the ladder, with Sutton right behind him, carrying the ten steel drills in a canvas sling.

When the pair was standing on the platform, the timekeeper waited until Penrose nodded to him. Then he glanced at his watch, his hand slowly rising into the air. A moment later he cried, "*Go!*" His hand came sharply down.

So did Penrose's sledgehammer to ring sharply against the steel drill which Sutton, kneeling, was holding tightly in both hands.

Sutton gave it a quarter turn.

Penrose swung the sledge.

Splinters of granite were caught in the mop rags Sutton had carefully placed in a circle around the spot where they were drilling.

Two minutes later, Sutton shouted, "Water!"

Water was poured into the hole in the granite. A thin wisp of steam hissed upward.

Sutton rose and moved gracefully to his left as Penrose's

body swiftly bent and he began to turn. Like two parts of one machine, adroitly attuned to one another, Sutton and Penrose exchanged places. In less than two seconds, the sledge was high above Sutton's head and Penrose was kneeling on the wooden platform with a new cold drill in his hands.

Sutton swung. Again. And again.

Sharp clangs split the air as the sledge in Sutton's hand hit the drill and drove it deeper and deeper into the granite.

Several minutes later, the two men, as gracefully and as swiftly as before, changed places again.

Sutton, bending over the drill in his hands, blinked as a piece of granite dislodged by the drill struck his cheek, but he did not falter.

"Now, my son!" Penrose shouted two minutes later. He swung his body down and around as Sutton rose, shifted, and took the sledge, raised it, and brought it down.

Water was again sloshed into the hole and again steam hissed from it as Sutton increased the speed of his strokes until he reached, as measured by the chanting men in the surrounding crowd, an amazing seventy-one strokes per minute.

Another minute passed and Sutton, during it, struck a total of seventy-nine strokes.

Again he and Penrose rapidly changed places.

Sutton, as he knelt on the wooden platform with the drill in his hands, shook his head and sweat flew from his face.

Sweat also slicked Penrose's face and spilled from the ends of his mustache as he pounded at the drill Sutton was gripping and turning after each blow of the sledge.

The crowd was quiet, awed by the skillful performance of the two men as they worked on. The timekeeper glanced at them, admiration in his eyes, and then back at the watch in his hand.

Sutton, on his knees and bent over, the drill in his hands, saw the hammer descend toward the drill. . . .

He knew it was going to happen but he nevertheless held

the drill firmly in place. When the hammer of the sledge slid off the side of the drill and struck his left hand, he gritted his teeth, but he did not let go of the drill. Instead, he gave it another quick quarter turn.

When Penrose saw the blood that quickly covered Sutton's hand, he went rigid, the sledge held high above his head.

"Strike, Jack!" Sutton shouted.

"Your hand, Luke, 'tis—"

"Dammit, man, *strike!*"

Penrose struck.

The crowd cheered.

Again Penrose hesitated, the sledge held high above his head.

"Come down, Jack!" Sutton shouted as he turned the drill and it slid in his bloody hand.

"One minute remaining!" the timekeeper called out.

"Change off!" Sutton shouted and dropped the drill. He seized the sledge and Penrose dropped down and grabbed a new sharp drill.

Sutton, blood running up his arm as he raised the sledge, struck and granite chips flew, most of them catching in the mop rags.

Water was poured into the hole and it mixed with Sutton's blood that had dripped down into it. Each time Sutton brought the sledge down, blood dripped from his hand.

"*Stop!*" roared the timekeeper.

Sutton dropped the sledge and, panting, sat down heavily on the block of granite as the official with the yardstick stepped forward and inserted it in the hole from which Penrose had wearily withdrawn his drill.

Penrose made his way over to Sutton and put a hand on his shoulder. "Oh, 'tis sorry I am, Luke, 'ow much I can't 'ardly tell thee."

Sutton looked up. "I'm alright."

The crowd was quiet, waiting.

The yardstick was withdrawn from the hole and shown to the timekeeper whose eyebrows arched.

He glanced at Sutton and Penrose a moment before calling out, "Thirty-eight and three fifths inches!"

The crowd erupted in cheers.

"Did thee 'ear that, old son!" Penrose shouted to Sutton at the top of his voice.

Sutton grinned.

Then, after they had climbed down from the platform, Penrose led Sutton to the nearby drugstore where the druggist quickly washed and then placed antiseptic on his injured hand.

"Anything busted, Doc?" Sutton asked.

"Doesn't seem so," the druggist replied.

Sutton and Penrose made their way back to the platform where the third team was vigorously drilling.

Sutton silently counted their strokes. He estimated that they were making somewhere over thirty per minute.

"You there!" a male voice called out and Sutton turned.

"Splendid job you both did!" said a man as he elbowed his way through the crowd toward Sutton and Penrose.

As the man came closer, Sutton recognized him as the mine superintendent who had hired Penrose to work in the High Stakes Mine.

Sutton nodded a silent greeting.

"I'd no idea you were that good at drilling," the superintendent declared, his eyes on Sutton. "Nor did I realize you were as strong as an ox. You're slender. It's deceiving."

Sutton started to turn back to the platform from which steady clangs were coming.

"I'd like to hire you," the superintendent said, catching hold of Sutton's arm.

"To do what?" Sutton asked, without turning, his eyes on the team sweating on the raised platform.

"Hard rock mining along with your friend here."

"Luke, now doesn't the good Lord provide for 'is lambs?" Penrose cried happily.

"You've just hired yourself a miner," Sutton told the superintendent.

"Report to work in the morning," the man responded.

On the platform, the timekeeper bellowed, "*Stop!*"

A little later, he called out, "Thirty-four inches exactly! The winner of this drilling contest is team number two— Penrose and Sutton!"

Cheers.

Penrose threw his arms around Sutton and happily hugged him.

"Hey!" Sutton protested, trying to free himself. "I already got me a bad hand, thanks to you. Don't go busting my ribs too."

"We did it, thee and me!" Penrose crowed, releasing Sutton and throwing his hat into the air. "We won!"

"Not bad," Sutton said with a grin, "for a fiddle-footed Cornishman like you and an old Texas stump-jumper like me. Not bad at all!"

CHAPTER 4

Early the next morning, Sutton and Penrose, both of them carrying tin dinner pails, arrived at the building that housed the hoisting works of the High Stakes Mine.

They joined the throng of sleepy-eyed men who were entering the huge building and, once inside, Sutton stared up in awe at the forty-foot ceiling and then, in astonishment, at the several large square openings in the wooden floor from which gushed great clouds of steam.

A bell sounded in the distance and Sutton turned to see a small hammer strike the bell again as the rope to which the hammer was attached was pulled by someone in one of the shafts below. The bell was, he realized, a signal because the large hoisting engines—each manned by an engineer who kept his eyes on the dial—abruptly roared into life.

"Those dials by the engines," Penrose said, "tell the engineers the location of the men below."

"All aboard, gents!" one of the engineers bellowed cheerfully and waved a beefy arm.

" 'Ere we go, Luke."

Penrose led the way to the cages which were suspended above the openings in the floor and Sutton, as he walked along behind Penrose, stared at the huge spools which, he estimated, were at least fifteen feet in diameter and around which were wound three-quarter-inch-thick cables of braided wire. As he watched, one of the spools began to turn, its cable unwinding. At the same instant, the cage full of men to which the cable was attached began to descend into the steam pouring up out of one of the mine shaft openings. An instant later, the cage disappeared from sight.

"We've got to go down into that?" Sutton asked Penrose.

"Into what, my son?"

"That's live steam pouring up from below."

"Ah, thee'll soon get used to it. Thee'd best strip off thy shirt. We're going down and once we get there we'll find it hot going."

But Sutton left his shirt on as he and Penrose stepped into one of the cages which was, Sutton was dismayed to find, nothing more than an iron frame with a solid floor and open sides.

"A man could fall off one of these contraptions real easy," Sutton commented and Penrose cupped a hand around one of his ears as the din that arose from the hoisting works and from the machinist's, carpenter's, and blacksmith's shops inside the building intensified.

Sutton repeated his observation, this time shouting it, and Penrose nodded somberly.

Suddenly, it seemed as if the world had fallen away beneath Sutton's boots.

The cage in which he and Penrose stood, along with several other men, began to descend at a dizzying speed into a limbo of half-seen candles flickering in the blackness, a limbo in which the half-heard shouts of men echoed, a limbo in which huge timbers flashed upward past the cage and then were gone, while the sound of picks striking stone threatened to split eardrums.

The shaft seemed to Sutton to be flying upward at a speed he found incomprehensible. He planted his boots on the floor of the cage as firmly as he could and reached out to grip one of the iron uprights of the cage.

Penrose seized his hand and pulled it back. "Keep thy hands and thy feet inside the cage!" he yelled. "Stand as close to the middle of the cage as thee can else thee'll 'ave a 'and or foot ripped off."

Sutton nodded, becoming aware of the intense heat as the cage continued to descend rapidly through the moist steam which was billowing up from below.

When the cage came to a halt at the fifteen-hundred-foot level, Sutton asked, "Where now?" and Penrose answered, "We follow the main drift over there. It runs north-south along the line of the lode."

As the two men walked, slightly hunched over to avoid striking their heads on rocky outcroppings in the uneven ceiling, Sutton noted the occasional crosscuts they were passing which ran east-west.

"What's that?" he asked Penrose, pointing to a vertical shaft.

"A winze," Penrose answered. "Those short shafts run up and down to connect with other levels of the mine. Mind your step there, Luke. Don't stumble over those tracks."

Sutton carefully avoided the narrow-gauge ore cart tracks.

"'Ere's our spot, my son," Penrose declared a moment later. He bent down, picked up a pick, and handed it to Sutton. "We'll start work here in this crosscut."

Sutton hefted the pick and, after flicking sweat from his forehead, swung it against the wall facing him, dislodging several large chunks of ore. He continued swinging the pick, while Penrose worked in the same manner beside him, and soon found himself standing in a pile of ore higher than the tops of his boots.

Around him, candles rested on rocky ledges. They flickered and threatened to go out as gusts of tepid air from the huge blowers placed strategically at various points throughout the mine swirled over and around him.

Dust rose and blew about, stinging his eyes and burning his throat. His injured hand throbbed and the bandage covering it soon grew gray, then black.

He continued working while, beside him, Penrose exchanged his pick for a drill and sledge with which he proceeded to attack the bluish-gray ore in front of him. "This 'ere, I'm told," he said to Sutton, "is the Big Bonanza. It runs all along the fifteen-hundred-foot level." He dislodged chunks of black ore and commented, "Sulphuret ore, that." A little later, he pointed to the place Sutton's pick had fractured the wall. "That's chloride ore, that steely-gray stuff. Thee can tell it by the pale green tinge it 'as in places."

Sutton stripped off his shirt and tossed it to the ground as filled ore carts rumbled past him toward the cages on which they would be hoisted to the surface. His sweaty torso glistened in the candlelight, giving him the look of a marble statue. He went on working, and sweating, occasionally coughing because of the ubiquitous dust.

"Jack," he said, "I'm just about drained of all my juices. Were you to serve me up on a platter, you'd find me done to a turn."

"'Tis 'ot 'ere," Penrose agreed. "They tell me that's because of the subterranean fires burning below the lode. But 'old on just a wee bit longer, my son. Then it will be time for us to go to the ice chamber."

"Ice chamber? If there's ice down here in this heat, I'll eat it."

"Thee will do that, I wager. Most men do."

A few minutes later, Penrose dropped his sledge and drill. "Come along, Luke."

Sutton followed him through the dim crosscut, out into the equally dim main drift, and on to a stoutly timbered square chamber just off the main drift. As Sutton entered its cool interior, he let out a sigh.

"Did I lie to thee?" Penrose asked as he seated himself on an empty wooden candle box. "There's water," he said, pointing to a cluster of wooden barrels. "And over there—ice."

Sutton used a tin cup to drink from and he filled and emptied it four times before he was satisfied. Then, taking a lump of ice from another barrel, he rubbed it over his chest and arms before sitting down next to Penrose and placing the rapidly melting lump in his mouth.

"'Alf hour on the job, then 'alf hour off in 'ere," Penrose said.

"It's hard to believe," Sutton said when the ice in his mouth had melted and trickled down his throat. "Paradise. Right next door to hell."

Several other miners entered the chamber and hurriedly availed themselves of water and ice from the barrels.

"That fellow has himself a good idea," Sutton said, pointing to a man wearing cut-off long johns, and Penrose nodded.

Sutton pulled his bowie knife from his boot and then pulled off his boots. He stepped out of his jeans and used his knife to cut off his long john bottoms at mid-thigh. He sat down again and pulled his boots back on.

A man's head appeared around the door of the chamber. "You two." He pointed at Sutton and Penrose. "You're malingering. You've been in here nigh on to an hour. Back to work, both of you."

Sutton was about to protest but Penrose said, "Yes, sorr. We're both on our way back right now, sorr."

The man's head disappeared.

"We've been here not more than ten minutes," Sutton said angrily as Penrose got to his feet.

"My son, don't antagonize the foreman. Let's go, Luke."

The miner, whose clothing style Sutton had imitated, remarked, "That's why we're ready to strike."

"One of the reasons," amended one of the other miners as he filled the tin cup.

The miner wearing cut-off long johns said, "They get more work out of us by cheating us of the time we're supposed to be able to spend here in the ice chamber."

"Come on, Luke," Penrose said.

Sutton, carrying his jeans, followed Penrose back to the crosscut where they had been working. Once there, both men resumed working and Sutton found his long johns—what remained of them—were soon thoroughly soaked with sweat. They clung to his skin as he worked doggedly on.

Ore carts, filled and on their way to the hoisting cages, thundered by. Others, empty, rolled past on their way deeper into the crosscut. The dust settled on the miners, turning them grimy as it blended with sweat and ran in dirty rivulets down their nearly naked bodies.

Sutton reached out with his free hand to dislodge a lump of chloride ore he had loosened. He let out a yelp and quickly withdrew his hand.

"I should 'ave warned thee, Luke," Penrose said apologetically. "This ore reaches a hundred twenty—a hundred thirty—degrees." He swung the pick he was using and, as it struck the outcropping in front of him, a stream of steaming water gushed out. He leaped backward just in time to avoid being scalded by the water.

When the stream had become a trickle, he raised his pick and was about to bring it down upon the wall when he hesitated. "Look there at that, Luke."

Sutton, who had also leaped backward when the hot water had gushed from the rock, moved closer to the wall and saw a thick mass of what looked to be precious stones glittering in the light of the candles.

"Iron and copper pyrites," Penrose declared as he stared at the crystal formation that glowed with a brilliant and colorful fire. "Pretty stuff," he commented and then swung his pick and shattered the crystalline structure.

Both men continued working, moving on a little later into an adjoining square set of short timbers neatly joined into a box-like frame. When it was time, they returned to the ice chamber and again they were hurried out of it by the mine foreman before their half hour was up.

Back at work in the square set, Sutton spoke to the miner working on his left. "What's all this talk about a strike?"

"Some of us are for it, some against," the man replied. "I'm for it."

"Why?"

"You're new here, aren't you?"

"I am," Sutton replied.

"You been to the ice chamber yet?"

Sutton swung his pick and nodded.

"Then you know how the foreman won't let us stay the whole half hours we're allotted in there. Did you know that three men in the past two weeks have died down here from heat exhaustion?"

"I can believe it."

"We've asked for a rise in wages from three dollars a day to three-fifty. Did you know that they cut our wages down to two-fifty in bad times?"

"Got a couple of questions for you," Sutton said as he continued working. "Who'd you ask for the rise in wages?"

"The foreman."

"He can raise your pay, can he?"

"He can."

"Then what did you do when he turned you down?"

"Well, we've been talking about what to do next."

Penrose said, "Such talk is ugly. Luke, thee 'as a job so thee won't go 'ungry. Be content with that."

The foreman suddenly appeared and announced that it was dinner time. When he had disappeared, the miners sat down where they were and began to open their tin pails.

The man Sutton had been talking to said, "My name's Bob Danvers."

"Luke Sutton."

"What do you think we should do, Sutton?" Danvers inquired and then bit into a thick sandwich he had taken from his lunch pail.

"Who's the owner of this mine?"

"A man named Roy Harding."

"Anybody been to talk to Mr. Harding?" Sutton took a meat pie Penrose had made for him from his lunch pail and began to eat it.

"We wouldn't dare bother Mr. Harding with our troubles," Danvers said quickly.

"Why not?" Sutton asked.

"Well, because—well, he's—" Danvers fell silent.

Sutton stared for a moment at tiny gleaming lights just beyond the edge of the candlelight and then he realized that he was looking into the eyes of rats. He was about to look away from them when one of the rats darted out of the darkness and seized a piece of bread that had fallen from Danvers' sandwich.

Danvers swore and swung a heavy boot which caught the rat and flung it against the wall. But it quickly got to its feet and fled squeaking into the darkness.

"Don't see why you fellows don't tell Mr. Harding about your grievances," Sutton remarked. "If anybody's to do anything about them, he strikes me as the man most likely to succeed in remedying them."

"Luke," Penrose said, "don't make trouble, my son. Do your work and keep your mouth shut."

Danvers said, "We don't get our full half hours in the ice chamber. They make us overload the cages when they're hoisting ore to the surface and, one day, one or more of us is going to get crushed when one of those cages comes crashing down on our heads. They won't buy enough pumps to keep all the water out of the shafts so that there are times when we're working knee-, nay, hip-deep in water down here. Oh, we've got grievances, we have. A whole long list of them!"

Sutton managed to catch Danvers' eye. He held it and, speaking loudly enough so that the other men seated nearby could hear him, said, "When I've got me a burr in my britches, I don't rest easy till I get it out. And if I got real sick I'd hunt myself up the best doctor I could find to cure me."

Danvers studied him. So did the other men. Finally, one of them said, "He's right, Bob. We've got to do something for ourselves."

"The Lord helps them that helps themselves," said another miner, his voice solemn.

"Send somebody to talk to Mr. Harding," Sutton advised. "Lay it all out in front of him."

"What if he won't listen to us?" one of the miners challenged.

"Make him listen." Sutton finished the last of his meat pie. Turning to Penrose, he said, "Jack, my own ma couldn't have made a tastier treat than that meat pie of yours."

Penrose smiled and said, "We Cornishmen who've 'ad the

boldness and brass to cross the pond and come to this country are fond of calling meat pies like the one you just ate 'a letter from 'ome.'"

Sutton returned Penrose's smile.

Danvers said, "They've taken to shutting down the blowers an hour before quitting time. We roast down here, we do, during that hour."

Sutton stood up. "Dammit, man, stop whining! Don't any of you—" he swept his hand around the circle of seated miners "—have the backbone to go to Harding and state your case? You've most certainly got one, there's no denying that."

"Maybe none of us does have the backbone," Danvers said thoughtfully. "Do you, Sutton?"

"'E's called thee, Luke," Penrose said. "Thee 'ad best back out while the backing out's still good or thee'll soon find trouble snapping at thy 'eels."

There was a sudden silence in the crosscut.

Sutton realized that the blowers had been shut off.

Danvers said, "They shut them off during dinner too. They say we don't need them seeing as how we're not working during dinner. It saves Mr. Harding some money."

"Danvers," Sutton said, "where might I be likely to find this fellow named Roy Harding?"

A spontaneous cheer went up from the circle of miners as Danvers gave Sutton Harding's address. One of them leaped up and slapped Sutton on the back.

Minutes later the foreman shouted an order that echoed through the shaft and crosscuts, and Sutton, like the other miners, closed his dinner pail and made his way back to work.

As he swung his pick and ore fell around his feet, he tried to block out the incessant thunder of the heavy ore carts as they went past him. He tried to ignore the dust that the blowers sent swirling everywhere. He paid no attention to his sweat which fell on the chunks of ore at his feet and almost instantly, because of the intense heat, dried there.

The remainder of the long day became for him a seemingly endless string of alternating half hours—one spent in the crosscut, the next in the ice chamber, the next back in the crosscut. . . .

It ended, finally.

Sutton wearily dropped his pick and proceeded to pull on his jeans and shirt. He walked beside Penrose, neither man speaking, out of the crosscut and down the shaft toward the cage that would lift them both up into the world of sunlight and cool breezes so far above them.

When they reached the spot where they would board the cage, they found it had been hoisted up. Still silent, they stood waiting for it to descend again.

"They care more about their damned fool tools than they do about us," a man beside Sutton grumbled. "They've hoisted up a bundle of drills to be sharpened by the machinist before us."

Sutton looked up the steamy shaft and was barely able to make out the floor of the cage high above him as it continued to rise.

Suddenly, he heard a heavy thud and then the clanging of metal against metal. "Look out!" he yelled at the top of his voice and sprang to one side. "Jack!" he shouted.

Penrose had been staring at the ground and, when Sutton shouted his name, he turned around.

Sutton leaped forward, seized him by the shoulders, and threw him to one side. He dived for cover himself an instant later.

The drills that he had seen falling from the cage when it swayed and struck an obstruction on one side of the shaft came clattering down, a deadly and merciless hail of metal.

Sutton stared, his teeth clenched, as the beveled point of one of the long drills struck a miner who had not moved out of the way fast enough. It plunged into his shoulder near his neck so deeply that only two inches of metal were visible.

The other thirteen inches were buried inside the hapless man's body.

He fell to the ground without uttering a sound.

Miners ran to him, knelt, and whispered fearfully among themselves. One finally rose and, looking up, shook his fist as the cage continued its ascent, finally becoming lost to sight in the steam that billowed in the shaft.

"Lord, that was a close call!" Penrose whispered as he stared in horror at the dead man lying not far away. "Were it not for thee, Luke, I might be dead now."

Sutton said nothing as he thought of what he had noticed back in the crosscut during the day. And now this, he thought. It'll be a wonder if any of us'll live if we keep on coming down here.

That night he paid a visit to the elegant two-story Harding home. He found that the name Harding was incised on a brass plate which was set in the center panel of the front door.

Proud man, Sutton thought as he knocked on the door. Wants the world to know his name.

"Yes?"

A maid stood in the open doorway. She wore a crisp black dress and her blond hair was topped by an even crisper white cap.

"I'm here to see Mr. Harding," Sutton told her. "It's important."

"I'm sorry, sir. Mr. Harding is not at home."

"You're sure about that, are you?" Sutton, his impatience growing, resisted the sudden impulse to boot the door open and search the premises.

"Who is it, Melinda?" A woman's voice, lilting and slightly husky.

"Luke Sutton!" Sutton called out.

"Sir," the maid began but fell silent as a woman of striking beauty appeared in the foyer wearing a green silk dress which had white daisies embroidered on its hem and high neckline.

"I'll see to this, Melinda," the woman said, her eyes on Sutton.

His were on hers which were such an icy blue that he did not notice Melinda withdraw.

"Mr. Sutton?"

"That's me. I came to talk to your—" What? Husband? Father? Brother? Sutton, momentarily perplexed, hesitated.

"My husband is not at home, Mr. Sutton."

"When will he be home? It's important that him and me have a talk together."

"Roy—Mr. Harding is out of town on business. He left here two days ago for San Francisco, as a matter of fact. I'm really not sure just when he plans to return. Is there something I can do for you, Mr. Sutton?"

"It's not likely."

Mrs. Harding's eyes seemed to narrow and Sutton was aware that she was appraising him with those cold blue eyes of hers. "Is there trouble at his mine?"

"There was. A man who was working in the High Stakes was killed today because nobody bothered to smooth out the sides of the shaft the cages ride up and down. The way I see it, more men might die if working conditions in that mine stay as bad as they are right now."

"I'm sorry to hear about—the death."

"I figured I'd best talk to your husband about the way things are in his mine and maybe about raising wages of the men he's got working for him."

"You're—just what are you, Mr. Sutton? A reformer? A troublemaker? One of the men agitating for a strike against the mine owners?"

"I guess you could say I'm a little bit of all of those things you named."

Mrs. Harding's hand rose to finger the delicate embroidery on her dress. "Are you a miner yourself, Mr. Sutton?"

"I am. In your husband's High Stakes."

"I see. Did someone force you to go to work there?"

"Nobody forces any man to work in the mines but—"

"Then the men are free to walk out at any time, are they not, and find employment elsewhere of a kind they deem more suitable?"

"Sure they are, but—"

"But most of the men continue to work in the mines. The pay is steady even if the working conditions can't, I suppose, compare to those enjoyed by a ribbon clerk or grain merchant."

"Mrs. Harding, there's talk—hot talk—of a strike. Now it makes sense to me for men like your husband to sit down with their workers and talk things out, maybe make some changes, compromise here and there. You say the pay is steady. Steady, maybe. Good, no ma'am. Things here in Virginia City are expensive. I've no doubt that men with families have to scrimp and pinch to make every dime go as far as two bits would—or even farther."

"Mr. Sutton, my husband has a saying, one he is very fond of using. 'Hungry hounds hunt best,' he has said more than once or twice in my hearing. I doubt that he would want to listen to your ideas for reform of the miners' working conditions or for raising their wages. You might do better were you to talk to the president of the Mine Owners' Association."

"What's his name and where can I find him—I mean right now, tonight?"

"His name is Mr. David Honeywell and he lives on the northwest corner of B and Taylor streets. Good evening, Mr. Sutton."

Sutton turned before Mrs. Harding could close the door on him and quickly made his way to the address she had given him.

The Honeywell residence was painted white and sported bright green shutters on its many windows. Above the round colonnaded entrance was a circular gallery which was bordered by a black wrought-iron fence.

Sutton went up to the front door and raised the brass knocker. He brought it down twice in rapid succession.

A moment later, the front door was opened by another uniformed maid who stared at his face, then at his clothes, and said, "Deliveries are made in the rear of the house— through the servant's entrance." She started to close the door.

Sutton lodged a boot between it and the jamb as the maid uttered a low protest. "My name's Sutton and I'm here to see Mr. Honeywell. You tell him that." He put out a hand and pushed the door open. He stepped into the foyer and closed the door behind him.

The maid, looking back over her shoulder once, hurried down the hall and disappeared.

Sutton looked about the ornately furnished parlor that opened off to his left and at the marble floor beneath his boots. Honeywell, he thought, is a man who knows how to live high off the hog.

The maid reappeared at the end of the hall. "Mr. Honeywell will see you in the library." She pointed to her right, and then fled through a door directly behind her.

Sutton strode down the hall and went through the door the maid had indicated. He found himself in a large room lined with filled bookshelves. A fire burned in the fireplace. There was a man seated in a wing chair facing him.

"Mr. Honeywell?"

"I understand your name is Sutton. I don't believe, sir, that I have had the pleasure."

"You haven't since you're not, I expect, in the habit of hobnobbing with the men who work this town's mines."

"You're a miner, Mr. Sutton?"

"Started work today in Harding's High Stakes. Heard talk.

About a strike. Thought I ought to come to see you and tell you what I heard so you could do what's necessary to keep the men on their jobs."

Honeywell smiled. "Let me tell *you* what you were about to tell me. May I?"

Sutton waited.

Honeywell rubbed his hands together and said, "The men want another fifty cents a day in wages. They don't want their wages reduced by fifty cents when a vein plays out and another one doesn't open up right away. They object to various cost-cutting measures that have been taken to increase the profitability of mines like the High Stakes. Yes?"

"You're right, so far. Add on that the men object to the fact that whoever's responsible for the timbering Harding's got down there's using more than one or two half-rotted pieces of wood. Add on that I noticed the clay that's mixed into the lode swells up when it's uncovered and air gets to it which makes it fill up the tunnels so working's not easy. Add on too that some of those square sets of Harding's aren't fitted snug enough up against the ore. They could cave in and kill any miner unlucky enough to be nearby when they give way."

"You are, obviously, an observant man, Mr. Sutton. But I believe these are matters that should be taken up with your mine's superintendent. His name is—"

"You could get Harding to order him to replace those rotted timbers I mentioned. To inspect every square set and fix those that're weak. To put men to hauling the clay out of the tunnels and crosscuts."

"Mr. Sutton, let me explain something to you. I do not oversee the day-to-day operations of my own mine, let alone Mr. Harding's. That is the job of my mine superintendent and the foremen under him. I have far more important things to do. There is stock in my mine to be sold. There are reports to be prepared. I must attend meetings of the Mine Owners' Association. So may I suggest that you—"

"Did you know a man was killed in the High Stakes today?"

"I did not. But the incident will be mentioned, I am quite certain, in the superintendent's weekly report concerning Mr. Harding's operations."

"Incident," Sutton repeated, making the word sound obscene. "That's what it is to you—a man gets a steel drill driven halfway through him and you call it an 'incident.' "

"Mr. Sutton, I am one man, the owner of one mine. But there is something you should know about the way I and the rest of the mine owners operate. We operate in concert, Mr. Sutton. Were I to raise my workers' wages, I would cause trouble for my colleagues. Were I to make certain operational alterations, that too would make trouble for the other mine owners, who all happen to be my friends, because their workers would soon be clamoring for similar changes. I will do this, however. I will see if the matters you have just mentioned to me may be placed on the agenda of a future meeting of the Association."

"That's real nice of you, Mr. Honeywell. Only thing is, that won't do the man with the drill driven into him much good. Nor is it likely to offer any aid or comfort to the man or men who might die tomorrow or the next day down in some mine on account of a cave-in."

"I appreciate your taking the time and trouble to come here and express your point of view, Mr. Sutton, but now—well, there are matters that demand my immediate attention. I'm sure you understand."

"Oh, I understand alright, Mr. Honeywell, I'll be moseying along now like you want me to do. But before I go I just want to tell you that you mine owners are likely to have a strike on your hands before long."

Honeywell cleared his throat, hesitated a moment, and then said, "Mr. Sutton, may I tell you something in confidence?" When Sutton nodded, Honeywell continued, "I and a number

of other mine owners are not averse to altering certain conditions in our mines, but Mr. Harding is unalterably opposed to
such changes since they would adversely affect the profitability of the mines."

"So why don't you fellows just rear up on your hind legs
and do what you want to do and to hell with Harding?"

Honeywell sighed. "Mr. Harding has managed to buy con-
siderable stock in a number of local mines, mine among them.
In fact, he holds a controlling interest in my mine, as he does
in two other mines. He has threatened to exercise that control
to our financial detriment should we oppose him in this matter."

"So it looks like Harding's the key to this whole thing."

"Why don't you have a talk with him?"

"I just came from his house. Harding's out of town. Talked
to his wife. Got nowhere with her. But I'll try again to talk to
him once he gets back here to Virginia City. Maybe I can
make him listen to reason."

"None of the members of the Mine Owners' Association
have been able to do that in the past, Mr. Sutton. I hope you
may succeed where we have failed."

"Well, I'll give it one first-class try, I can promise you that."

CHAPTER 5

The next morning, over a breakfast of salt pork and beans, Sutton, in response to Penrose's query, told him about his talk with Honeywell the night before.

"Well, thee did the best thee could, Luke. Now, put the matter behind thee and look to the future."

Sutton looked up from his plate in surprise. "Put the matter behind me? Jack, I've only just started to try to change things."

Penrose, frowning, drank some coffee and then, putting down his cup, said, "Luke, thee would do well to mind thy own business. If some of the men want to strike, let them. I've 'eard talk about what 'as 'appened at other mines in this country when the men went on strike. The owners of the mines brought in scab labor. Sometimes they even called in militiamen to break the strike. And what those soldiers broke, in addition to the strike, were not a few 'eads. Thee doesn't want thy skull split, now, do thee, my 'andsome?"

"I don't, Jack, but something has to be done. You know that as well as I do."

"What 'as to be done is every man 'as to look out for 'imself. 'E 'as to step lively, say a prayer, and keep 'is eyes wide open so 'e won't get 'urt."

"That's not good enough for me," Sutton said. "What would it take to make a few changes to improve safety in the mines? Not much. I'm going to see to it that changes are made."

"Doesn't thee know what might 'appen once 'tis known what thee are doing, Luke? Thee will be fired, that's what."

"Maybe."

"'Tis a sure thing." Penrose emptied his cup. "What is it thee are planning to do next?"

"It might be best if you didn't know, Jack. That way, you wouldn't be tempted to tell on me."

"I'd never tell! I swear to thee I wouldn't, Luke!"

"Just joshing, Jack. No need to get all fired up." Sutton rose.

"'Tis early yet, Luke."

"Got something I want to do before I start work today. See you later."

Once outside, Sutton made his way to the office of the *Territorial Enterprise* only to find when he arrived that the door was locked. Well, he thought, it was a chance I was taking.

Looks like Mr. William Wright doesn't get up with the chickens. Maybe he keeps banker's hours.

Sutton was about to head for the High Stakes when he saw a man striding down C Street toward him.

No miner he, Sutton thought, not with that cloak he's wearing billowing out behind him like a bishop in full sail.

As the man came closer, Sutton, recognizing him, said, "Morning, Mr. Wright."

Wright halted and studied Sutton. "I remember you."

"Name's Luke Sutton. I was in your office the other day."

"Inquiring about a friend of yours, as I recall."

Sutton let it go.

"Adam Foss, wasn't it?"

Sutton nodded. "Want to talk to you, Mr. Wright. But I'm not at all sure how to begin."

"Just begin," Wright suggested.

"You know anything about the working conditions down in the mines?"

"I know they are, by and large, deplorable in most cases. I've done some prowling about down in the mines myself and I find them fascinating. Those are brave men down there, every last one of them. Or perhaps they are foolhardy. Sometimes, I've noticed, it is exceedingly difficult to tell the difference between those two qualities."

"I talked to Mr. Honeywell last night," Sutton said, still not sure whether he could expect any cooperation from Wright concerning the plan he had formulated.

"Pillar of the community," Wright commented and Sutton thought his voice had sounded a little tart.

"Tried to talk to Roy Harding, but he's in San Francisco."

"What about?"

"About getting things changed down in the mines. About saving lives."

"You're a crusader, are you, Mr. Sutton?"

Sutton grinned. "Mrs. Harding had the notion I'm a troublemaker and now you're looking to stick a label on me too."

"You obviously have something in mind, Mr. Sutton. It involves me?"

"It could if you'd see your way clear to let it."

"Tell me how I fit into your plans."

Sutton did.

When he had finished, Wright let out a low whistle.

"The miners aren't only in danger every day of their lives," Sutton continued. "They also aren't paid a decent wage for the work they do."

"I've heard rumors that the men are talking of a strike. That could mean trouble."

"It could," Sutton agreed. "What I have in mind is avoiding that trouble and it could be done—with your help, Mr. Wright."

"Call me Bill, Luke." Wright paused thoughtfully and then, his eyes gleaming, said, "I've been in a few fights—in print, that is—since I came here. Tweaked a few noses, I have, in my time. Now what you're proposing might very well be a way of making the mine owners not only sit up and take notice of the men they employ and the needs of those men, but it might also prompt them to make some necessary changes in wages and working conditions. I'll do what you suggested, Luke!"

"Hold on a minute, Bill. It's dark down in the mines, as you well know since you've been down in them. All we got down there is candles and a handful of lamps. Will that give you enough of the light you'll need?"

"No," Wright said firmly and then, seeing the discouraged expression on Sutton's face, hastened to add, "but we'll get tin reflectors, a flint and steel, and a supply of magnesium. That will guarantee us enough light. When do you want me to start?"

"Bill, you strike me as a man who doesn't let any grass grow under his boots."

Wright smiled and said, "I'll get Barney O'Brien and the two of us will go down into the High Stakes this morning."

"You won't have any trouble getting down?"

"I doubt it. I'll tell anyone who asks that I'm writing a story on the mine. What I won't tell them is the kind of story I'm writing. I shan't have any trouble. The men know me because of the way I've prowled about down there, especially on the upper levels of the mine—the tunnels that have played out and been abandoned.

"Luke, you should see them! It's another—a very weird world. Down in those deserted and dreary old levels, I've seen fungi of monstrous growth and most uncouth and uncanny form. They cover old posts in great moist, dew-distilling masses, and depend from the timbers overhead in broad slimy curtains, or hang down like long squirming serpents or the twisted horns of the ram. They—"

Sutton interrupted. "I'll meet you at the foot of the shaft on the fifteen-hundred-foot level and show you what you ought to see. What time'll you be down, Bill?"

"Ten sharp."

"I'll be there to meet you—at ten sharp."

Sutton was.

As the cage shot down the shaft and came to an abrupt halt, he, without a word, beckoned to Wright and the man standing beside him, who was carrying a large box camera and a scarred satchel.

He made his way along the main drift and then turned right into a crosscut.

When he finally halted, Wright asked, "Is this the place?"

Sutton nodded and pointed to a nearby square set that was not set flush against its neighbor.

"Luke, this is Barney O'Brien, the paper's photographer."

After the two men had shaken hands, O'Brien proceeded to unpack his satchel. He placed tin reflectors at strategic spots and candles, which he lit, directly in front of them to increase the amount of illumination provided by two nearby lamps.

Then, after preparing his plates and loading his camera, he said, "Ready."

"Shoot the floor over there after you've got the square set," Sutton directed. "Be sure you show how that clay's crumbled and weakened the ceiling. Then, get a shot of these timbers right here." Sutton patted them. "Be sure you show how bad they're rotted at their bases."

Sutton and Wright stepped back. O'Brien, humming to himself, opened his shutter and at the same instant struck a flint with his steel. There was a bright burst of light as the spark he had struck ignited the magnesium he had prepared.

After photographing the unstable joints of the square set, he aimed his camera at the clay that was sifting down from the ceiling and repeated the process. He photographed the rotting timbers and was about to obey Sutton's instructions to shoot the deep sump of steaming water at the far end of the crosscut when the foreman came storming down it.

"What's going on here?" he thundered.

"I'm William Wright," Wright said quickly, smiling benignly at the foreman. "I'm writing a story on mines and mining for the *Territorial Enterprise*. This is Mr. O'Brien, my photographer. And this gentleman—one of your miners—has been kind enough to pose for me to give our pictures, which will illustrate our story, some human interest."

"You're not allowed down here!" the foreman bellowed.

"There is some law against my being here?" Wright asked, his voice pleasant, his smile still in place.

"No, not exactly. But it's—it's dangerous."

"Is it, sir?" Wright asked. "Well, have no fear. If I'm injured I shall not hold the company liable in any way. Would you like me to sign a waiver to that effect? I shall be more than happy to do so."

"This is highly irregular!" the foreman spluttered, looking around as if for help of some kind.

"Sir," Wright said, "would you stand over there? We'd very much like to take your picture as well as Mr. Sutton's. Luke, over there, both of you." Wright pointed. Sutton moved next to the sagging post Wright had indicated. The foreman joined him, taking up a position directly in front of the post, unwittingly hiding it from the camera.

"Stand in the light," Sutton told him. "Otherwise, your friends won't know it's you. You'll just show up as one more shadow in the picture."

The foreman ran his fingers through his thick hair, stepped to the opposite side of the timber, and thrust his hands into his pockets, staring straight at O'Brien's camera.

Sutton winked at Wright who turned to the photographer. "Proceed, please, Mr. O'Brien."

O'Brien promptly sparked more magnesium which flared into life and burned brightly.

The foreman was still grinning at the camera when O'Brien closed its shutter and removed the plate from it.

"That should be quite enough, I think," Wright said. "I want to thank you, sir," he said to the foreman, "for your admirable patience. If you'll tell me your name, I'll include it in the caption that will run beneath this picture."

As Wright and the foreman conferred and O'Brien began to pack up his gear, Sutton, unnoticed, moved down the crosscut and began to swing a pick, dislodging chunks of ore which fell to the ground and lay sparkling around his boots.

Two days later, Sutton sat at the table with Penrose in the shanty they shared, and said, "Bill Wright didn't write this story. Somebody else did—a man named Dan DeQuille. But it's good it is. Listen to this, Jack." He smoothed out the copy of the *Territorial Enterprise* he had been reading. "'The pictures accompanying this article tell far more than mere words can. They show in graphic detail the dangers the men face who brave the mines day after day. These dangers have been pointed out to your reporter by a man employed in the High Stakes Mine, Mr. Luke Sutton. Note the rotting timbers. Examine for yourself the unstable ceiling and the improperly joined square sets. All these things may mean death to the men who work underground in the Comstock Lode. As if to confirm that fact, Mr. Martin Josephson, foreman on the fifteen-hundred-foot level of the High Stakes Mine, told this reporter in unequivocal terms that it was dangerous for him to be in the mine. Clearly, the foreman was correct. And, just as clearly, it is also dangerous for the men whose livelihoods are dependent upon them having to expose themselves to such perils on a daily basis. . . .'

"DeQuille goes on," Sutton said happily, "to write about how the miners need an increase in pay. He says the company ought to issue gloves to the men on account of the way our wooden pick handles get too hot to hold on to down there."

"'Ow did Wright know that?" Penrose asked.

"I told him, that's how he knew. This story tells how they shut off the blowers during dinner and about how we don't get to spend a full half hour at a stretch in the ice chamber. It says it would be—well, listen to what it says. 'The men should be required to work no more than fifteen minutes before being allowed to cool their burning bodies and wet their parched throats in the ice chamber for fifteen minutes before returning to work. . . .'

"This is how he winds up his story, Jack. Listen. 'The mine owners, we humbly suggest, must be, in the light of the atrocities outlined in this article, considered at best negligent where the safety and well-being of their workers are concerned and, at worst, criminally liable for their failures in this important regard.'"

"'Tis trouble thee are asking for, Luke. Why did thee let them take thy picture and plaster it all over the front page like that?"

"Why not?"

"I'll tell thee why not. It will lead to thy losing thy job, that's why not."

"I don't think so. If they went and fired me now, it would only work against them, make them look worse than they do already."

Penrose, scowling at the tea in the cup before him, was silent.

"Don't worry about me, Jack. I can take care of myself."

Penrose looked up at Sutton. His scowl gave way to a smile. "'Tis an old woman I'm being, the way I'm meddling in another man's business. I'll not anymore, Luke."

"You weren't meddling, Jack. You were giving me what's probably good advice and I appreciate it."

"But thee'll not be taking it?"

Sutton grinned. "Not this time. But don't give up on me, Jack. Keep trying to turn me toward being sensible."

"That's one of the things a friend's for."

"And you're one of the best friends I've ever had, Jack. Why, thanks to you, I'm two hundred and fifty dollars richer right this very minute than I'd otherwise be."

"Thee more than carried thy weight in that double-jacking contest, Luke."

Sutton got up from the table and removed his hat from a wall peg. He clapped it on and said, "I'm going out, Jack. See you when I get back."

"'Tis likely I'll be resting these weary bones of mine in my bed when you get back."

"In the morning then."

Sutton left the house. He made his way down C Street through the pall hanging over the town which was composed of smoke, alkali dust, and shadows, and when he reached the office of the *Territorial Enterprise,* he went inside.

"Hallo, Bill!" Sutton called out as he stood just inside the door of the empty office.

A door opened and a young man appeared. "Mr. Wright's not here. I'm his printer's devil. Is there something I can do for you, sir?"

"You can tell me where I might find him."

"He has a room at the International Hotel. He might be in it."

"Much obliged."

When Sutton arrived at the International Hotel, he went inside and asked the desk clerk for the number of Wright's room. When he had it, he leaned over the desk and beckoned to the clerk. As the clerk leaned toward him, he asked, "Are a man's life and limbs safe in one of those elevators you got over there?"

"Most certainly, sir," the room clerk declared, drawing back again, apparently unaware of Sutton's attempt at humor. "They're hydraulic elevators and completely safe."

"Then I guess I'll take a chance on riding one of them," Sutton said and headed across the lobby.

When the operator of one of the elevators threw open the folding iron gate, Sutton stepped inside and the gate closed behind him.

"Floor, sir?" asked the operator.

"Five. And be sure you stop before you hit the roof."

The elevator operator's face remained impassive as he swung a lever and the cage began to rise.

"Mind if I ask you something?" Sutton inquired. "Don't a man's legs go bad on him if he lets himself be boosted up and down too many times in a machine like this?"

"Your floor, sir," the operator said and opened the gate.

Sutton stepped out into a thickly carpeted hall and made his way down it until he found the numbered door of Wright's room. He knocked on it.

"Come in!" Wright called out from behind the door.

Sutton opened the door and stepped into a richly furnished room which contained a walnut bed, several chairs, and a marble-topped dresser. Nottingham-lace curtains covered the windows.

"Luke! This is a surprise."

"Your printer's devil told me I might find you here. Wanted to thank you for that article in the paper. Good writer, your man DeQuille. Wouldn't mind meeting him."

Wright smiled. "You already have."

Sutton stared in surprise at Wright.

"I am Dan DeQuille," Wright declared, still smiling. "It's a nom de plume I use."

"Well, like I said, that was one real rouser of a story you wrote and I sure do appreciate it. It ought to stir up something of a storm or I miss my guess."

"I fervently hope that it does. I'm in sympathy with the miners and I hope my story will pave the way to the swift redressing of their legitimate grievances. Let's have a drink, Luke. What do you say?"

"Sounds like a fine idea to me," Sutton said and followed Wright out of the room.

Downstairs, at the bar adjoining the ornate lobby, Wright ordered beer; Sutton, whiskey.

"Let's toast our efforts, Luke," Wright proposed, raising his glass. "Here's to the health of our enemies' enemies!"

Sutton thought of Adam Foss. He raised his glass, catching Wright's eye. Still thinking of Foss and wondering how long it would take him to catch up with the man, he said, *"Go mbeirimid beo ar an am seo aris."*

Wright stared at him, perplexed.

Sutton grinned. "My pa was Irish through and through.

He was also a drinking man. That's a toast he taught me. Learned it, he said he did, in the old country when he was but a boy. It's Gaelic. In English, it comes out, 'May we be alive at the same time next year.'"

"I trust we both will be," Wright said, raising his glass until it clinked against Sutton's.

Both men drank.

Fifteen minutes later, following a desultory conversation which was frequently interrupted by solemn silence, Wright announced that it was time for him to go.

"I've a long day tomorrow," he remarked. "And before I retire for the night I must write a letter to my wife and children in Iowa."

"Didn't know you had a family, Bill."

"I do. But mining towns aren't for them although they do seem to entice me—Virginia City does, at any rate. Can't seem to tear myself away from it. As a Washoe widower, I've been living in boardinghouses and hotels for years now. Well, I'll give you a good night now, Luke."

A man's voice suddenly interrupted them. "You there, Wright!"

Wright and Sutton both turned at the sound of the man's voice.

"Ah, Mr. Manning," Wright said as the superintendent of the High Stakes Mine came storming up to the bar.

"That was a nasty piece of work, Wright," declared Manning. "A vicious piece of work."

"You are referring, I take it, to my newspaper article about the conditions in your mine."

"You know damned well I am." Manning's voice rose as he announced, "It won't change a thing. I'm sure Mr. Harding has no intention of raising the workers' wages. Nor does he intend to change the way the mine operates."

"He might reconsider," Sutton said softly, "if he finds himself with a strike on his hands."

Manning turned to face Sutton. "Sutton, you're fired as of right now. Mr. Harding's orders."

"Is that a fact?"

"It is. Mr. Harding ordered your dismissal along with the foreman who allowed the pair of you to do your dirty work. Mr. Harding has also given me orders to fire on the spot any man who complains either about the wage he is being paid or the conditions under which he earns that wage."

"If you follow through on that order," Sutton suggested, "you and Harding might find the only thing you've got down in those tunnels is rats. And rats aren't much good at mining ore."

"There will be no strike," Manning snapped, "because the men need their jobs. It's that simple. How long do you think they'd last without their weekly wages? Not long, I can assure you. But, even if they did strike, the High Stakes would continue to operate. We would simply import men—"

"Scabs!" Sutton snapped back.

"—to work the mine. If necessary, to protect our interests, we would call in the state militia. The governor would be sympathetic to our request. Perhaps you know that Mr. Harding contributed quite lavishly to his last election campaign."

"Were you to bring in scab labor, Manning," Wright said, "you'd be risking violence."

"But the firepower, Wright, would be heavily on our side of the fence, and you know it." Manning turned and stalked from the bar.

"Luke, I'm sorry about you losing your job."

"I'll get along, Bill. What happened, well, it might turn out to be a blessing in disguise. I don't fancy getting myself caught in a cave-in and maybe killed."

"If there's anything I can ever do for you, Luke, just ask. Will you do that? You're a decent man and—well, good night again."

When Wright had gone, Sutton refilled his glass and stood

leaning on the bar and thinking about what had just transpired. He'd lost his job. So be it. He still had one, a more important one. He had to find Adam Foss, wherever . . .

His attention was diverted from his thoughts by loud laughter erupting in the room. He turned his head and saw a man at the bar, still laughing loudly, seize the braided pigtail of a frail Chinese and pull it hard.

The head of the Chinese jerked backward. His hands rose in an attempt to dislodge the grip of his tormentor but he failed to do so.

The Chinese, Sutton noted, was an elderly man. He was wearing a brightly embroidered black silk jacket that reached below his hips and silk pantaloons, which revealed his white socks and low-cut black leather slippers.

"Have a drink," ordered the man as he suddenly released his hold on the man's pigtail. He reached out to the bar and picked up a full glass of whiskey.

"No, please," said the Chinese, backing away.

Another man stepped up behind him, blocking his retreat.

"You won't drink it, maybe you'll wash in it," declared the man who held the glass in his hand. He threw the contents of the glass into the face of the frightened Chinese.

The old man cried out as the alcohol stung his eyes. He clawed at his face and tried to make his way out of the bar.

But the man who had thrown the whiskey seized his pigtail and jerked him backward.

The old man lost his balance and fell heavily to the floor.

Sutton got up and strode over to the bar. Reaching down he gripped the old man's hand and felt him cringe as he did so. "On your feet," he said and pulled. When the Chinese was standing blinking beside him, he addressed the two troublemakers. "You two jaspers had enough fun for tonight?"

The two men looked at one another for a moment and then the one who sported a thick mustache slowly shook his head.

"We don't let niggers in here. Chinamen ain't nothing but bleached niggers. We're going to teach him a lesson."

"We'll teach you one too," said the second man, his small eyes glaring at Sutton, "if you don't get out of our way."

"I'll be glad to get out of your way," Sutton said amiably. "Me and my friend here were just leaving." Sutton, gripping the old man's elbow, started to steer him toward the door leading to the lobby.

A heavy hand landed on Sutton's shoulder and spun him around. A fist landed against the side of his head and he staggered backward.

The small-eyed man who had struck him moved in on him, and Sutton, releasing the elbow of the elderly Chinese, stepped swiftly to one side. He reached down and grabbed the man's outflung arm, swung him in a semicircle, and then, giving the man a mighty shove, sent him careening into the oak bar. The man moaned and slumped down, arms akimbo, his body draped over the brass rail between a pair of spittoons.

Sutton turned swiftly and found the man with the mustache heading for him, both of his fists raised. The man moved to the right as Sutton brought his fists up. Sutton moved to the left. Both men moved in a circle for a moment and then Sutton's opponent lunged forward. His right fist glanced off Sutton's shoulder. Sutton swung his left and his uppercut caught the man beneath the chin, snapping his head backward. He followed up the blow with a quick one-two, both blows, as he had intended, landing just below his opponent's rib cage, knocking the wind out of the man.

He moved slightly backward as the man, recovering but wheezing now, crouched low and came toward him, both fists ready. He dodged the man's right jab, feinted with his left, and then landed a solid blow on the side of the man's head which sent him stumbling backward.

The man collided with a table. It fell to the floor and so did the man.

Before his opponent could rise, Sutton was on him. Seizing the man's coat in both hands, he hauled him to his feet. Then, swiftly drawing back his right arm, he delivered another uppercut and heard something crack as his fist connected with the man's jaw.

Suddenly, Sutton's knees buckled as the man he had floored earlier jumped him, landing on his back, his right forearm encircling his throat.

"Give it to him, Hank!" the man holding Sutton yelled.

Hank got up from the floor and, as blood trickled from the left corner of his mouth, drew back his left arm and let his fist fly. It caught Sutton on his nose from which blood began to flow.

Hank let out a whoop of delight and began to pummel Sutton's body. A moment later, he moved closer and Sutton put out one booted foot, caught Hank behind his knee with the toe of his boot, and threw the man off balance. Sutton seized him and shoved him backward. At the same time, he doubled over and sent the man behind him flying over his back to hit a table, splintering it.

Sutton, a cold fury possessing him now, moved in on both men. As Hank got to his feet, Sutton gave him a right and then a left, the second blow turning the man around. He reached out with his left hand, turned Hank toward him, and landed a right uppercut on the man's jaw which dropped him. He turned and went for Hank's companion. He let the man get to his feet and then struck a succession of blows, each one more fierce than the last, all of them landing on the man's body, battering it mercilessly and unrelentingly.

The man's eyes rolled up in their sockets. His body arched and, as Sutton took a step away from him, he crumpled to the floor.

Sutton stood there for a moment looking down at the two

unconscious men. He flexed his aching fingers slowly and then took another step backward. He turned and went to where the elderly Chinese was standing not far from the bar, his eyes wide, his trembling lips betraying his fear.

"Come on, old fellow," Sutton said to him, wiping his bloody nose with the back of a hand. "We're getting out of here now."

Both of them walked through the door, across the lobby, and out into the smoky night.

"I want to thank you, sir," said the Chinese in a soft, well-modulated voice. "I do not like to think of what might have happened to me had you not come to my aid."

"Those old boys would have gone on tormenting you some more but then they would've gotten tired of their game and let you go. You're fine now. Best you head on home."

"Sir."

Sutton turned expectantly toward the old man.

"Your nose—it is bleeding. Come home with me. My grand-daughter will take care of you."

"I'll be fine."

"You have done an old man a great favor. Will you not allow him the chance to do a small favor for you in return?"

"Put that way, I don't see that I've got a choice in the matter. Let's go."

CHAPTER 6

"My name is Kee Chin," said the elderly Chinese as he walked north on B Street with Sutton.

"Luke Sutton."

"It is not much farther, Mr. Sutton."

"Luke'll do fine."

"That house is the one in which I live," Chin said, pointing at the two-story building partway up the slope of Mount Davidson. "It is a boardinghouse owned by a woman of my people. I was fortunate to find it. As you know by now, we Chinese are not always welcomed by whites."

"You been living in Virginia City long, have you?" Sutton inquired as they reached the house and climbed the stairs to its porch.

Chin, bending to unlock the door, said, "No, not long. We arrived here from San Francisco only two days ago, my granddaughter and I. I did not want her to come, but she would not let me travel alone."

Sutton followed Chin into the gas-lit hall and then up the steps.

Chin opened a door that was just beyond the second-floor landing and bowed Sutton into the room beyond it.

Sutton found himself in a large bedroom which was sparsely furnished and immaculately clean.

A door in the wall near the bed opened and a young woman came through it. She ran to Kee Chin and kissed him lightly on the cheek. She said something in Chinese to him and was answered in the same language.

Sutton found himself admiring her slender figure that was clothed in a white silk sheath which reached from the base of her throat to her ankles. She was, he decided, a very attractive woman, with black eyes and straight black hair which curled up around the lobes of her ears. Her skin was smooth, her nose straight, and her lips pert above a small chin.

"My granddaughter, Mei-ling," Chin said.

"Pleased to meet you, miss."

Mei-ling bowed slightly to Sutton.

Chin spoke to her again in Chinese and she turned and left the room. When she returned several minutes later, she was carrying a porcelain bowl and a clean cotton cloth.

"Please sit here," she said to Sutton, indicating a tall-backed wooden chair. When he had done so, she tore the cloth, and proceeded to wash away the blood from his upper lip. Then, using the remainder of the cloth, she made a cold compress and placed it across the bridge of his nose. "Lean back," she said, her voice a mere whisper, a soft breezy sound in the otherwise quiet room.

Again Chin spoke to her rapidly and at length in Chinese as Sutton rested the nape of his neck against the high back of the chair.

Mei-ling listened to her grandfather and then, when the old man finished speaking, she turned to Sutton and said, "My grandfather tells me that you saved his life. I thank you for that. I am deeply grateful for what you did to help him."

"Your granddaddy tells tall tales. I didn't save his life. Just swatted away a pair of flies that started pestering him, is all."

"From what he has just told me, you did, I gather, much more than merely swat those two flies. He says you quite thoroughly smashed them." Mei-ling smiled at Sutton.

"What started all the trouble back at the hotel?" Sutton asked Chin.

"I went there to inquire about the Eureka Mine," Chin replied. "In fact, I came here to get whatever information I could about the mine wherever I could. I own stock in the mine, stock which will, upon my passing, belong to Mei-ling."

"I thought that mine owners or their underlings put out regular information on their operations."

"Some do," Chin said, nodding. "Some don't. The information given out by those who do is not always easily decipherable. Luke, I was worried enough about my investment in the Eureka to come here all the way from San Francisco to find out everything I could about the mine."

"Because of this," Mei-ling said after opening a dresser drawer and removing a piece of paper which she handed to Sutton.

He removed the compress from his nose and sat up in his chair. He unfolded the paper and read what turned out to be a letter from the Board of Directors of the Eureka Mine. The letter had been addressed to Kee Chin in San Francisco.

"This seems plain enough," he said, looking up at Chin. "They want to buy new equipment and are assessing their stockholders to pay for it."

"Mr. Sutton—"

"Luke," Sutton said to Mei-ling.

She smiled and said, "Luke, this is the sixth letter in as many months that my grandfather has received, each of them asking for more money."

"It takes money to run a mine," Sutton commented.

"But," interjected Chin, "I have so far seen no return on my investment. I think that is strange. Don't you?"

"It might be and it might not be. Like I said, it takes money to run a mine."

Mei-ling said, "My grandfather paid five thousand dollars in cash for his one hundred shares of stock when he first bought them. Since then, he has been assessed a total of an additional two thousand dollars."

Sutton looked down at the letter in his hand. "Now they want another five dollars a share from each stockholder which means you have to come up with five hundred more dollars." He hesitated a moment and then looked up at Chin. "If you're feeling uneasy about all this, why don't you tell them you won't keep on paying?"

Chin lowered his head and folded his hands in front of him. "If I do not continue to pay, I will lose my stock. Such was the agreement I signed when I originally made the stock purchase."

"Well, now, don't that put things in a different light?"

"You can understand my concern at this point," Chin said. "But I have not met with much success in my initial inquiries, as you saw tonight at the hotel."

Mei-ling spoke to her grandfather in Chinese.

Chin glanced at Sutton and then back at Mei-ling. He shook his head.

"What'd she say, Chin?" Sutton asked.

"Mei-ling wondered if you could make inquiries concerning the Eureka on my behalf. But that would be an imposition."

"No, sir, it wouldn't be."

Mei-ling's face brightened and she clapped her hands. "Then you will see what you can find out for us, Mr.—Luke?"

"Sure I will. Glad to. I'll start first thing in the morning. I got to ask some questions of my own around town and I can ask about the Eureka at the same time." He rose.

"Please don't go," Mei-ling said. "Not yet. I'll return in a moment. Please sit down, Luke."

She left the room again and during her absence, Sutton noticed, the room seemed to have dimmed. When she returned she carried a tray on which rested a china teapot and three china cups which had no handles. She placed the tray on a table. Then, gracefully and silently, she poured the tea, handing the first full cup to her grandfather, the second to Sutton.

He drank from his cup. "I never have tasted tea as good as this before."

"It is imported from China," Mei-ling told him. "It is quite refreshing."

It is, Sutton thought, drinking from his cup, his eyes on Mei-ling. And so are you.

When Sutton awoke the next morning, he heard Penrose moving about in the kitchen. He got up and used the water that remained in the bucket beside his bed to wash and then he dressed and went into the kitchen.

"Thee'd best hurry, Luke. 'Tis getting late."

Sheepishly, Sutton said, "You were right, Jack."

"Oh, was I now?" Penrose placed a plate containing fried salt pork and two eggs in front of Sutton. "About what?"

"I was fired last night."

Penrose's face turned mournful. He said nothing.

Sutton told him about his encounter with the mine superintendent the night before.

Penrose poured coffee into a cup and placed it beside Sutton's plate. "Well, there are other mines in need of good men like yourself."

"Thanks, Jack." When Penrose gave him a puzzled look, Sutton said, "I mean for not acting smug. You did warn me."

"I'll keep my ear to the ground, Luke, and should I 'ear of anything—an opening of any kind—I'll let thee know first thing. Well, I'm off. See thee tonight."

Sutton nodded and, as Penrose left the house, he proceeded to finish his breakfast. When he had done so, he left the house and strode purposefully down C Street, heading for the office of Billet and Ferris, the mining claims agents. As he entered the office, a young man seated behind a desk looked up and asked, "May I help you, sir?"

"Maybe you can. I'm interested in the Eureka Mine. In who happens to own it. Thought you might know."

"I'll be glad to look it up for you, sir." The young man opened a drawer of his desk, took out a ledger, and deftly flipped through the alphabetical listing until he found the entry he had been searching for. "Did you want the name of the original owner or the name of the man who owns it now?"

"Before I answer that one, let me ask you a question first. When did the Eureka change hands?"

"A little over a year ago—in November of eighteen seventy-five."

"Then I'll be wanting the name of the present owner."

"The Eureka is currently owned by Mr. Roy Harding."

"Well, now, it sure is a small world, isn't it?"

"Beg pardon, sir?"

"Never mind."

"The Eureka was a good producer in its time," the young

man commented. "But you know how it is. A rich vein is struck and mined for all it's worth but once it's gone—well, sometimes there's not another one to be found."

"The Eureka's played out, is it?"

"Well, I wouldn't want to commit myself on that score, sir. It did, in its time, do rather well and there is, of course, always the chance that it will do well again. Mr. Harding may begin operations at any time and who can say what he will discover. The Eureka isn't another Bullion Mine."

"Not sure I follow you."

"The Bullion is in the very heart of the Comstock Lode and it went down two thousand seven hundred and twenty-five feet, but not a trace of silver was ever found in it. The mine was a total loss to its owners and investors."

"Where exactly is the Eureka Mine located?"

The young man got to his feet and rounded his desk. "I can show you on this wall map," he said, beckoning to Sutton. "It's right here." He placed an index finger on an outlined square that appeared next to other claims marked on the huge map. "It's just east of the Sutro Tunnel, as you can see."

"I thank you for your time and trouble. I've just one last question. Where's mining stock traded here in town?"

When the clerk had given him directions, Sutton made his way to the stock exchange and went inside to find himself in the midst of what, at first glance, appeared to him to be a saloon brawl.

Men were everywhere. They ebbed and flowed like a tide. They shouted to one another, waved papers at one another, called out price quotations.

Sutton grabbed the arm of one harried-looking shirt-sleeved man and said, "What's stock in the Eureka selling for?"

The man, after shouting, "Twenty dollars per on the Ophir," consulted a notebook he pulled from his pocket. He ran a finger down page after page before looking up at Sutton and answering, "That stock's pretty much inactive. There hasn't been any trading in it for some time now but, if you're interested in buying Eureka stock, I can get you a current quotation."

"Not interested. Just curious."

"May I suggest, if you're in the market to make a quick profit, that you buy up as many shares as you can in the High Stakes."

"A move like that might make me rich?"

"It depends on the magnitude of your investment, of course." The man leaned closer to Sutton and whispered, "There's been a run on the stock of the High Stakes for the last few days."

"A selling spree?"

The man laughed heartily. "On the contrary. The stock— every share of it being offered for sale—has been snapped up. When I first noticed the trend, I did some checking. What, I wondered, accounted for the sudden interest in the High Stakes. Granted it's been a good steady producer. Nothing extraordinary, you understand. But—"

"You did some checking."

"Yes, I did. I noticed that the Thor Tool Works was the principal buyer. Now I happen to know that Thor Tool is owned by Roy Harding. Roy Harding, as you may know, owns the High Stakes."

Sutton waited and, when the man beside him winked, he said, "I'm not sure I see what you're getting at."

"I believe Harding is buying up all of his stock that he can get his hands on. Why, you ask. I'll tell you. I think he's hit a rich strike and is keeping it quiet. Meanwhile, he's buying up his stock—at twelve dollars a share—and then, once he announces the strike, the price of High Stakes stock will soar and he'll sell dear what he bought cheap. It's a common practice."

"How sure are you that he's made a rich strike?"

"I'm not sure at all. But when you've been in this business

as long as I have you learn to recognize the possible meanings of the tremors that run through the stock market from time to time. Of course, the whole thing is a gamble. But then so is life itself, is it not?"

"It is that. I'll consider what you just told me and maybe be back to buy a few shares in the High Stakes myself. Thanks for talking to me."

Once outside, Sutton made his way to the Eureka Mine where he found exactly what he had been expecting to find— a total lack of activity. The hoisting works stood silent. Ore carts sat rusting on their tracks. There were no mules or men visible. He was about to leave when a man emerged from the hoisting works. Sutton went up to him.

"You work here?" he asked.

"Watchman."

"Looks like the mine's shut down."

"Any fool can see that. It hasn't been worked in a year. Longer, if my memory serves me right."

"Now that seems funny."

"Nothing funny about it. A mine that's not working means men without jobs."

"What I meant was, I own stock in the Eureka," Sutton lied. "I've been being assessed a whole lot of money lately for new equipment and the like and yet you tell me this mine's deader'n a dodo. Doesn't figure."

"It might figure. Maybe whoever owns it's going to start operating again. Or maybe whoever owns it figures he can make money without doing any actual mining, if you know what I mean."

"I think I do. Now you tell me if I've followed your trail. An owner of a mine like the Eureka—one that's pretty much played out—he knows it but he buys it anyway so he can assess his stockholders for more and more money which he pockets, with them none the wiser."

"It's been known to happen here on the lode and other places too—like in the California goldfields."

"A man might've thought that would be against the law."

"What law? There's no law to tell a man he can't sell stock in his own mine. There's no law that tells anybody not to buy that stock because it might be worthless. It's a case of caveat emptor, buying mining stock is."

"Caveat emptor?"

"That's French. Or maybe Eyetalian. It means buyer beware."

"Uh-huh. Well, it's been real nice talking to you."

Sutton left the watchman and went immediately to the office of the superintendent of the High Stakes Mine.

As he entered it, Manning, who had been poring over the many papers piled high on his desk, looked up, frowned, and exclaimed, "I told you you were fired. Now, get out of here, Sutton!"

"I'll do that. Soon's you pay me what you owe me for the work I did here."

Grumbling, Manning glared at Sutton and then, with evident reluctance, took an iron cash box from a drawer and counted out a sum of money which he threw down on the desk. "Take it and clear out. I don't want to see you again, Sutton. You're nothing but trouble."

Sutton picked up the money, counted it, and then pocketed it. "Bought some of your mine's stock today," he lied pleasantly. "I guess you've been on the buying side too now that the High Stakes is really about to pay off."

"What are you talking about?"

"About that new vein you struck. About how Harding's been buying every single share of his own stock that comes on the market as fast as ice melts in hell."

"How did you find out about that vein?" Manning, his face reddening, suddenly got to his feet. "I don't know what you're talking about. Get out!"

Sutton left the office, satisfied that what he had believed to be true was indeed true. He smiled to himself as he thought of how he had tricked Manning into admitting outright that a rich vein had been discovered in the High Stakes. Luck, he thought. Comes to me about once a year, like Christmas. Still smiling as he made his way down into Virginia City, he was aware that his trick wouldn't have worked had he not spent most of the morning asking questions and getting answers like those he had gotten from the broker in the stock exchange.

His smile vanished as he thought of Kee Chin and Mei-ling. They'd been bilked, and badly. Now it was his sorry task to tell them so. He didn't relish doing it. But, he thought, what he had to tell them had a positive aspect to it. He would at least be able to keep Kee Chin from throwing good money after bad. Maybe more than just that, he thought. Maybe I can get Chin to put his money where it just might do the old man some good.

Turning thought into action, Sutton returned to Kee Chin's boardinghouse and was warmly welcomed by the elderly Chinese.

Once seated in Chin's room, Sutton proceeded to outline what he had discovered about the Eureka Mine.

Chin interrupted him to ask, "Then my stock is of no value, Luke?"

"Looks that way, Chin. Harding, like I said, bought up the Eureka knowing full well it was played out. He figured to make his money by assessing his stockholders time after time for as long as they'd stand still for it."

"I have been a fool," Chin declared sorrowfully, and Mei-ling, who was seated beside him, reached out and took his hands in hers.

"Gathered some other news during my wanderings," Sutton announced. "News that might interest you, Chin."

"What is it, Luke?" Mei-ling asked, hope brightening her voice as she gazed intently at Sutton.

He told her and Chin what he knew about Harding's efforts to buy up as much of the High Stakes stock as he could. He concluded his account by remarking, "Once he lets the news out about the new vein he's found, High Stakes stock will sky-rocket and he can make himself a handsome sum by selling off at the higher price all he's bought up."

"You think," Chin said thoughtfully, "that I should buy High Stakes stock now."

"All I'm saying," Sutton said, "is that it looks like a good gamble to me. You said you were being assessed another five hundred dollars for the Eureka and I figure now you'll be backing out of that deal. You could, if you want to take an-other chance, put that five hundred into High Stakes stock and hope for the best—hope that what I think's true really is."

"But if it isn't—" Mei-ling turned from Sutton to her grand-father.

"We would have lost our five hundred dollars in any event," Chin reminded her. "I was prepared to pay it to Mr. Har-ding." He patted Mei-ling's hand. "Once again, I believe we are in Luke's debt, child."

Mei-ling glanced shyly at Sutton who rose and said, "I'll be going. See you again sometime soon, I hope."

Mei-ling went to the door with him. "My grandfather is right, Luke. We are deeply in your debt."

"Not at all, Mei-ling. I just did your granddaddy a friendly turn or two, is all."

Sutton bade her good-bye and made his way toward C Street. When he reached it, he walked north, lost in his thoughts of Adam Foss. He made up his mind to pay a visit to Gold Hill. The town, he knew, was really a part of Virginia City, separated from it by only a ridge. The man who had tried to gun him down, he thought, had said that Foss was in Virginia City. But I've scoured this town, he thought, and turned up neither hair nor hide belonging to Foss. Maybe the would-be assassin had considered Gold Hill a part of Virginia

City. Tomorrow, Sutton thought. I'll climb over that ridge to-morrow and see if I can find out anything about Foss in Gold City. Or, he quickly amended, maybe I'll head over there as early as tonight.

He halted at the edge of a crowd. A man wearing a stove-pipe black hat stood on a box in the center of the crowd shouting out names and prices.

It took Sutton only a moment to realize that what he was witnessing was the auctioning of mining stocks that had belonged to delinquent holders. He stood there, listening as the auctioneer alternately bullied and coaxed the crowd into buying.

"Nineteen dollars!" a woman cried out and Sutton turned, surprised that a woman would be among the bidders.

His surprise intensified as he recognized the woman.

"Who'll bid twenty?" cried the auctioneer. "A giveaway, gents—and lady—at twenty dollars a share. A veritable steal. Twenty, am I bid twenty, do I hear twenty—" He looked around the suddenly silent crowd. He sighed and then clapped his hands together. "Sold for nineteen dollars a share to the wife of one of Virginia City's outstanding citizens, Mrs. Roy Harding. Mrs. Harding, if you'll be so good as to see my assistant, he will accept your check and turn over the certificates to you. Now, then, gents, I have several small holdings in the Eureka Mine which I'm sure you'll—"

A muted mumbling ran through the crowd as Sutton watched Mrs. Harding make her way toward the man stand-ing on the ground next to the auctioneer's box.

"No takers?" cried the auctioneer, simulating incredulity. "Not one?"

So word about the Eureka's gotten around town, Sutton thought. It's a good thing Chin came to check out his hold-ings when he did or he could go on paying for maybe years before news of Harding's swindle ever reached the stock ex-change in San Francisco.

Sutton noticed that Mrs. Harding was coming toward him. As she approached, he touched the brim of his hat to her and said, "Afternoon, Mrs. Harding."

She looked up in surprise, frowned, and then said, "Mr. Sutton."

"Yes, ma'am. Nice seeing you again." Sutton noticed the purplish bruise below her left eye and she noticed him noticing. She turned aside and was about to make her way around him when he said, "Mind if I walk along with you, Mrs. Harding?"

She didn't reply as they left the auction and Sutton was aware of the fact that she kept her face averted from him.

"Your husband home from San Francisco yet?"

"Yes, he is."

"When would it be convenient for me to come calling on him?"

Mrs. Harding suddenly gripped Sutton's arm. "Would you be good enough to escort me?"

For a moment, Sutton didn't understand what her question meant. Not until she gestured in the direction of the saloon across the street. He offered her his arm and she took it. Together they crossed the street and entered the saloon she had indicated.

Sutton drew up a chair for her and she sat down at a table. "What'll you have, Mrs. Harding? I'll go get it for you."

"Whiskey."

Sutton nodded, turned, and headed for the bar at the far end of the room.

When he returned to the table, he sat down and filled the two glasses from the whiskey bottle which he had brought with him. "I'm surprised you recognized me," he said, "seeing as how we only met that one time. Your health, Mrs. Harding." He raised his glass to her.

As if she hadn't heard him, Mrs. Harding drank from her

glass. When she set it down again it was more than half empty.

Her blue eyes, Sutton noticed, darted around the room as if she were expecting to be accosted at any moment. She looked at the door, away from it, and then back at it again. She nervously patted her hair and then adjusted the brim of her hat, so that it rested low on her forehead.

She looked at the door again and said, "I'm afraid I've done you a disservice, Mr. Sutton."

"I hadn't noticed."

"Outside a moment ago—when we were leaving the auction—" A faint trace of a smile appeared on her face. The corners of her lips lifted but her eyes remained impassive. "Didn't you wonder why I so suddenly requested your company in this—this place?"

"Well, you did take me a bit by surprise."

"My husband."

"Your husband? What's he got to do with us being in here?"

"I just saw him approaching us. I didn't want to encounter him. But, since you *did* want to meet with him—the disservice I mentioned, Mr. Sutton."

"I see." Sutton watched her hand slowly rise to her face and her fingers delicately touch the bruise beneath her eye. "My explanation for why I did what I did," she said so softly that Sutton almost didn't hear her words.

"Your husband, he did that to you?"

Mrs. Harding nodded. "With his fist. You can readily understand now why I chose not to meet him on the street out there. I avoid him as much as I possibly can."

"He ever haul off and hit you before?"

Mrs. Harding hesitated a moment before answering, "Yes. Several times recently. Roy and I—we've not been getting along with one another for some time now. Until recently we had merely argued. But lately—matters have begun to take a rather ugly turn, as you can see."

Sutton smiled.

"You find my story amusing, Mr. Sutton?" she asked angrily, her eyes flashing.

Sutton's smile vanished. "Beg pardon, ma'am. I had a stray thought. I was remembering what that auctioneer called your husband. An outstanding citizen, I think he said. Wonder what he'd call him if he knew how you got that black eye."

"Have you had any success in your recent efforts, Mr. Sutton?"

"My recent efforts? Oh, you mean my trying to change a thing or two about the way the owners run their mines around here. Nope. Haven't even gotten as far as the barn door let alone all the way inside as of yet."

"Do you think there will be a strike?"

"There might be one. It begins to look like that's the only way things're going to get changed."

"I hope there is one."

Sutton drank from his glass and put it down. "You're yearning for somebody to cause your husband some trouble?"

"If there was a strike, he'd be liable to lose money—perhaps a substantial sum. Roy cares a great deal about money. It seems to be the only thing he does care anything about. But I have no grounds to complain really. I married him two years ago mainly because he had money. Oh, I found him attractive enough. But quite frankly, Mr. Sutton, my overriding motive for marrying him was his money and not his occasional rather crude display of tenderness toward me. You see, I was born dirt poor, lived poor, and was beginning to believe that I'd die poor. So I came to Virginia City—" She raised her glass to Sutton, emptied it, and giggled. "What was I saying? Oh, yes, about coming here to Virginia City. I was working as a saloon girl when I met Roy and decided he was the way to that better life I'd always dreamed about. He wasn't." She picked up the bottle and refilled her glass. "I'm feeling much less nervous now," she commented as if she were talking to herself. "But I'm also feeling, I'm perfectly willing to confess, a trifle tipsy."

"You could leave Harding."

"Not without money, I couldn't." She laughed bitterly. "My husband sees to my material wants but he is not lavish with his money beyond that—not where I'm concerned. But what little money I've been able to scrape together—I pawned some gold jewelry only the other day—I've been putting to good use."

"Speculating in stock?"

"Yes. Others have made money that way. Perhaps I can too. If I'm successful—then I can bid Roy a not very fond good-bye." She gave Sutton a lopsided grin. "I've talked too much about myself and my problems—and to a virtual stranger at that. Tell me about yourself, Mr. Sutton. Have you always been a reformer? I'm afraid I wasn't very sympathetic to your point of view when you came calling. I trust you will overlook my rudeness. Living with a husband like mine can make a woman rude—or worse."

"You sure do seem bound and determined to slap a sign on me that may or may not fit me. Does it make you feel comfortable to pigeonhole people?"

"Life is less unpredictable that way. But, please. Tell me about yourself. Where do you come from? What have you done with your life? What do you dream about?"

"That's a tall order, answering all those questions. I come from Texas. Haven't been back there in some time. I've done little with my life when you come right down to it. The same as most men, I guess. I've done some drifting and some cowboying. Been here, there, and all around the corral. Dreams? The only thing I dream about is finding a man named Adam Foss. And killing him."

Mrs. Harding didn't seem shocked by Sutton's harsh words.

She drank from her glass. "Those aren't dreams, Mr. Sutton. They're nightmares."

"Reckon you're right. They are mostly."

"Where are you staying while you're here in Virginia City?"

"With a friend I met on the train coming here. His name's Jack Penrose and he's got a little place that used to belong to his brother up on North C Street."

"Do you plan on remaining in Virginia City?" she asked with sudden earnestness.

"Well, I heard that Foss is—or was, at least—in Virginia City. I'm trying to find him."

"But you haven't found him yet?"

Sutton shook his head.

"Perhaps you never will."

"I will. Here. Or someplace else. Sometime."

"I asked if you were planning on staying because I know something that you should know, although I probably shouldn't tell you."

Sutton waited for her to continue.

She hiccupped. "Scuse me." She patted her lips with one hand and then winked at Sutton. Leaning over the table, she whispered melodramatically, "I heard my husband talking to that stuffed shirt Dave Honeywell. The pair of them were talking about—guess!" She giggled, and then jabbed a finger against Sutton's chest. "*You!*" She emptied her glass and continued, "Something about some newspaper article. I've not the slightest idee—idea—what *that* was all about.

"But I am sure that my husband is a ruthless man, one who gets what he wants, one way or another. Mostly he buys what he wants. You know, the way he bought me. Anyway. What I'm trying to say—what *am* I trying to say? No, don't interrupt. I remember. Roy'll kill me if he ever finds out I warned you." Unsteadily, she began to refill her glass.

"Warned me about what?"

"Roy and Dave said something about getting you out of

their way. About keeping you from making any more trouble. Luke—you don't mind if I call you Luke since we're friends now? Good. You can call me Opal. Luke, I think you'd be a lot happier—safer too if you take my meaning—somewhere other than in Virginia City."

"I appreciate the warning, Opal. But I'm not ready to leave town just yet."

"Because of that man—what's his name?"

"Adam Foss."

"You're staying on to run him down?"

"I am."

"What if my husband and some of his hired hands run you down first?"

Sutton shrugged.

CHAPTER 7

The earsplitting shriek of a mine whistle woke Sutton two days later from a nightmare about hordes of faceless gunmen who fired over and over again until Dan Sutton's body lay bloody and lifeless in a gray world beneath a sunless sky.

He grimaced and swung his legs over the side of the bed, the gunmen gone but not forgotten.

Penrose, he thought. He's still not home. He's been missing since the morning I left here to go to Billet and Ferris, mining agents. Was Penrose off on a bender? Some mysterious errand? Sutton rejected both ideas as he dressed. Maybe he'll turn up tonight, Sutton thought as he pulled his boots on, with some real wild story to tell me about what he's been up to.

As Sutton put coffee on to boil, someone began to pound on the door. He went to it and opened it to find himself facing a man with an ashen face whose lips opened and then closed wordlessly.

"What's wrong, Danvers?" Sutton asked, recognizing the man he had talked with in the High Stakes while he had been employed there.

"Sutton—" Danvers swallowed. He took off his hat.

"Out with it, man!"

"It's Jack."

"What about him?"

"He's hurt awful bad, Sutton. He got caught in a cave-in about an hour ago, him and three other men."

"What happened?"

"From what I heard, Penrose and the other three were working in a new tunnel. It's said to be rich in ore. Somebody told me that, when Harding heard about the strike, he ordered a few men locked up in the new tunnel so word about the strike wouldn't get out till he was good and ready for it to get out. Trouble was, they didn't put a timbering crew to working in the new tunnel and Penrose and the others had to use the post and cap method to keep the roof from caving in. It didn't work. We got them all out but they're busted up real bad, every last man of them."

"Penrose?"

"His chest is crushed and he's got a fractured skull. He wants you, Sutton. He sent me here to get you."

"Come on!" Sutton sprinted across C Street, Danvers running some distance behind him.

It took him less than ten minutes to reach the High Stakes and, when he did, he fought his way through the thick crowd that had gathered in front of the hoisting works, his mind racing, only partially conscious of the wailing of a woman and the muttered cursing of several men.

He found Penrose lying on his back with his eyes closed near the entrance to the hoisting works. Next to him lay another man over whom a kneeling priest in black cassock and white Roman collar was murmuring words as he administered the sacrament of Extreme Unction and bent his head to hear the injured man's words which wheezed from between his lips as he made his last confession.

Sutton, staring at the gaping wound on Penrose's forehead, was momentarily immobilized. But then, forcing himself to look away from the ugly cavity that was littered with fragments of shattered bone and through which part of Penrose's brain could be seen, he rushed forward and knelt down on the ground.

"Jack, it's me. Luke."

No response.

Sutton reached out hesitantly and touched Penrose's hands which lay folded upon his crushed chest.

Penrose moaned softly. His eyes opened, but only partially. He fought to focus them. "Luke?"

"Here, Jack. Right here."

"Ah, my 'andsome, thee came, did thee?"

"We'll get you a doctor, Jack." Sutton started to rise.

"'Tis no doctor I'm needing now, Luke. One's been to see me. So 'as the minister. And now thee." Penrose's eyes closed and then slowly opened again. "My 'ouse—do with it what thee will, Luke."

"I'll find the doctor. There'll be something he can do for you, Jack. He'll—"

"Does thee want to do something for me, old son?"

Sutton nodded. "I'll go get the doctor—"

"I was wrong about things, Luke. About the mine and the way things are down there. The men . . . one of them who was locked up along with me . . . five children, Luke. Five! He lost a leg, they tell me. Crushed to pulp, it was. Luke, make things better. Do what thee started out to do. For the men. For me. It would be a way of remembering me." Penrose tried to smile. His features collapsed and he groaned in pain.

"I'll remember you, Jack."

"Do, Luke, while thee tries to keep more men from dying down there in the dark," Penrose whispered softly and then coughed, a wet retching sound. He squeezed his eyes shut. "I'm glad thee got 'ere in time to—to say good-bye, Luke."

Sutton heard his own teeth grinding together.

"There's a thing I'd 'ave thee do for me, Luke."

"Name it, Jack. I'll do it."

"Write a letter to my mother in Cornwall. Tell her what 'as 'appened to her two boys—to Richie and me. Her address— thee'll find it on a scrap of paper in my satchel."

"I'll write to her, Jack. You can count on me."

"Ah, Luke," Penrose sighed, looking up at the sky. " 'Tis not dying that's so hard for a man to do. 'Tis the leaving of good friends such as yourself that makes it all so full of pain."

"Jack, I've got to go get the doctor. I—"

"There is another thing thee could do for me, if thee've a mind to, Luke." Penrose swallowed hard but bloody saliva slid from between his lips and down his stubbled chin. "Lay me to rest beside Richie. Will thee do that, Luke?"

Sutton wanted desperately to lie, to tell Penrose that things would be alright, that the doctor would come and perform his miracles, the ones which would close the gaping red hole in Penrose's skull and inflate again the dying man's ruined chest. "I'll do it, Jack," he said and, when Penrose smiled weakly up at him, he fought back his tears but a few fell into the dust in which he knelt. And then his grief gave way to a wild rage which coursed through him in a boiling tide.

Penrose's right hand rose and reached out, trembling.

Sutton seized it, held it tight. He was still holding it tightly when Penrose, seeming to wink as his eyelids flickered and then closed, died, his head lolling to one side.

Sutton released his hold on Penrose's hand and got to his feet.

The priest, he realized, was gone. The man lying next to Penrose was also obviously dead now. The woman who had been wailing had fallen silent. Men were beginning to move away. A wagon rumbled up and Sutton stood, his expression grim, staring at the pine coffins piled in the wagon's bed.

Suddenly, he turned and raced toward the entrance of the hoisting works. He scrambled up to the top of a stacked pile of timbers and let out a yell.

When the dispersing crowd turned toward him, he beckoned. "Listen to me," he yelled. "All of you. Come closer." He waited until the crowd had gathered around the pile of timbers and then said in a loud voice, "How long are you men going to put up with this? How long are you women going to have to go on living in dread of hearing the mine whistle that tells you there's been another accident and that your husband, your son, or your brother may be among the dead or injured? That man—" Sutton pointed to Penrose's body "—was a friend of mine. He's dead. Maybe some of you don't know why. Well, I'll tell you why. He's dead, my friend is, because of greed. The greed of men like Roy Harding who locked those men in his secret tunnel just so's he could make more money.

"Harding's been buying up stock in the High Stakes. You all mark my words. He'll sell it now when word of the new vein gets out as now it must and will.

"Which one of you—" Sutton let his eyes roam from face to face in the crowd "—will die or be maimed on account of the greed of men like Roy Harding? You?" He pointed to a man at the edge of the crowd and the man seemed to shrink away from him. "You?" He pointed to another man who looked down at the ground. "When will you men learn to stand up and fight instead of just talk?"

"You married, mister?" a man shouted from the thick of the crowd.

"I'm not," Sutton answered.

"Well, I am!" the man shouted back. "I've got a family to feed. It's all well and good for the likes of you to talk about fighting back. You've got nothing to lose."

"I worked this mine before I was fired," Sutton shouted back. "I had my *life* to lose just as you do every day you go to work. My friend lost his life today and I'll tell you something about him. If he could stand up now—if he could come back from the dead he'd point a finger, he would. He'd point it at *you!*" Sutton pointed to the man who had questioned him. "He'd accuse *you* of having a hand in his getting killed because you got yourself a wife and family to feed. But who'll feed them if you're the next to die down in the High Stakes?"

When the man didn't answer, Sutton continued, "Will Roy Harding feed them? Will the Mine Owners' Association feed them? You—every last one of you—you've all got to think this thing through and, if you do, you'll see I'm right. The only way to stop the dying is to fight back the only way you can. *Strike!*"

"No!" someone roared from the crowd. "They'll never let us come back to our jobs if we strike!"

"They'll bring in scab labor!" someone else shouted.

The crowd began to break up.

"Wait!" Sutton shouted. "You're good hardworking men. Strong men! You can fight the mine owners and you can win!"

"What we'll win," a man shouted angrily, "is empty bellies
—our own and our wives' and our young 'uns'!"

A cheer rose from the rear of the crowd.

When it died down, a woman approached the pile of timbers on which Sutton was standing and held up a hand to
him. "If you would be so kind, sir," she said and Sutton took
her hand and helped her climb up beside him.

She turned to face the crowd. "I don't know this man," she
began in a firm voice. "But I know that what he says makes
sense. Many of you know me so you know I'm not an
educated woman. But I am a woman who can use the little
bit of brains the good Lord saw fit to give me and I say that
you men—and you women too—have to stop living the way
you've been doing. The way me and my man and our brood
has too. You heard my husband ask this man beside me if he
had a wife. My husband missed the point. This man—" she
gestured in Sutton's direction "—has a *life,* as each of you
men have. He doesn't want to lose his. You don't want to lose
yours. But you've got to fight for what's decent for yourselves
and your families.

"Martin," she said, her eyes riveted on the man who had
first questioned Sutton. "You know I love you and you know
how much. We've had good years together. I want *more*
years, Martin. I don't ever want to hear that whistle blow and
come running out here to find *you* lying there." She pointed
to where Penrose's body and the body of the man near him
still lay. "I daresay there are other women here who feel the
same way that I do."

"There are!" a woman cried out. "I'm one of them!"

"I'm another!" cried a woman near her.

Other women took up the refrain.

"What's it to be then, men?" Sutton yelled. "What are you
going to do with the courage every last one of you has? Use it
down in the crosscuts? Or use it to strike the High Stakes

and every other mine around here until you win a decent wage and safe working conditions?"

The crowd was silent for a moment and then a man stepped from it and took up a position beneath Sutton's makeshift platform. "I'm a gambling man," he announced soberly, to the crowd. "My wife says it'll be the death of her one day. But this time I figure she'd want me to gamble so I'm going to gamble on a strike."

"Who else'll join the fight?" Sutton yelled.

A woman at the front of the crowd took the hand of the man standing next to her and led him up to the pile of timbers. "John will," she said simply, looking up at Sutton. "Won't you, John?" she asked, turning to the man standing somewhat sheepishly beside her.

"Well," he said, "I reckon I'd rather fight the mine owners than my wife." Smiling, he held up a hand to Sutton.

Sutton hunkered down and shook it vigorously.

As he straightened, the crowd broke into a roar and then into a chant "Strike! *Strike!*"

"Get the news down into the tunnels!" Sutton shouted. "Get the men up here and let's get ourselves organized! Danvers!"

"Yo!"

"Send somebody to tell the engineer inside to signal the men to come up out of the tunnels. Get somebody else to make sure they're all hoisted out. Then get everybody out here and we'll draw up a list of what we want from the mine owners."

Danvers left to carry out Sutton's orders and, while Sutton waited for the men from the tunnels to join the throng outside the hoisting works, he helped the woman beside him climb down from the pile of timbers.

"I sure do want to thank you for your help, ma'am," he told her when they were both on the ground once again. "If you hadn't've spoken up when you did, I think the men would have just walked away on me."

"Will it work, Mr.—"

"Luke Sutton."

"Do you think the strike will accomplish what we all want, Mr. Sutton?"

"I have high hopes that it will."

As the woman left to rejoin her husband, Sutton made his way to the office of the mine superintendent.

"You're asking for trouble again," Manning declared as Sutton entered the office. "I heard you out there getting my employees all worked up."

"You got paper? A pencil?"

"I wouldn't give you my dog's droppings."

"That's fine with me. It means I'll just have to take what I want." Sutton walked around the desk and pulled open a drawer.

As he did so, Manning made a grab for him. Sutton, as he pulled open another drawer, threw an almost absentminded right uppercut that sent the superintendent reeling backward to fall over a filing cabinet.

"Get out of here, Sutton!" Manning roared as he struggled to his feet.

"I'm getting," Sutton said pleasantly, waving several sheets of blank paper and a pencil he held in his hand.

Outside again, he was joined by Danvers who told him that the miners were all present, the tunnels deserted. He climbed up on the stacked timbers again and called for attention.

When the crowd had quieted, he said, "We'll make us a list of demands. Now, what's to be first on the list?"

"A rise in wages!" a man shouted. "From three to three-fifty dollars a day!"

"Make it five," Sutton declared. "That way, we'll have room to back down some if we have to—as far as four if we have to. That sit alright with you boys?"

A roar of approval went up from the crowd.

Sutton wrote on the paper as one demand after another was agreed upon. Finally, he held the paper high above his head and shouted, "This ought to do us. We're asking for better pay. For the blowers to be left on all the time any men are working in the mine. We want regular inspections of the square sets and other timbering for safety's sake. We want pumps to empty the sumps down there and a crew to take out the crumbled clay that's blocking some of the crosscuts. We want a fifteen-minute on, fifteen-minute off in the ice chamber set-up instead of a thirty-thirty-minute basis as it is right now."

Another cheer.

"Danvers!" Sutton shouted. "Pick a handful of good men and send them around to the other mines. Have them try to get every miner in Virginia City to join us."

"It's as good as done!" Danvers yelled back, smiling broadly.

"Danvers, wait!" Sutton shouted. "Take this!" He leaped down from the timbers and handed the sheet of paper with the miners' demands written on it to Danvers. "After you send your men around to the other mines, write out a copy of this. Take one to Roy Harding and give the other one to Dave Honeywell. Tell Honeywell that, as president of the Mine Owners' Association, he's the one to get the ball rolling. Tell him we said that if he don't get the ball rolling and rolling fast, him and a lot of other owners are going to be hurting before too long!"

"What are you going to do, Sutton?" Danvers asked.

Sutton glanced at Penrose's body lying on the ground not far away. "Got me some burying to do. But I'll be home by tonight. You come by and tell me how things went, will you?"

When he had filled the grave which adjoined that of Richie Penrose, Sutton took a candle and matches from his pocket.

Kneeling on the ground, he lit the candle and burned an epitaph into the wooden cross he had nailed together:

Here lies Jack Penrose
Good Man. Good Friend

Then, after using a rock to pound the wooden cross he had made into the ground at the head of the grave, he made his way down the slope of Mount Davidson and into Virginia City.

He went directly to the office of the *Territorial Enterprise* which he found to be in an uproar. Wright, in the middle of a number of scurrying men, was shouting orders in order to be heard over the muted thunder of the press coming from the rear of the building.

"Luke!" he shouted when he spotted Sutton standing just inside the door. "You heard the news?"

"About the strike?" Sutton shouted back as he moved toward Wright.

"No. I know you know about that since you're its ringleader. I mean about the stock of the High Stakes."

"It's going up, I'd guess."

"Skyrocketing!" Wright exclaimed. "Harding is going to be a millionaire before this is all over."

"Bill, I want you to write an editorial about the strike. Tell the people of Virginia City why the miners struck, what they want, all of it."

"You're too late!"

"Too late?"

"I'm way ahead of you, Luke. Wait right here!" Wright ran to a door in the rear of the office and disappeared through it. When he reappeared a moment later, he was waving a page of newsprint. "Read this!" he commanded and thrust the paper into Sutton's hands.

Sutton scanned the page, then read the editorial Wright

pointed out to him. "Not bad," he said when he had finished reading. "Couldn't have done better myself."

"It's time a few noses were tweaked around here," Wright declared happily.

"Not to mention a few butts booted into the bargain," Sutton said, grinning.

"We'll have the powers that be in Virginia City on the run in no time," Wright said. "It's about time too."

"Keep on giving it to them, Bill. It's a comfort to have the power of the press on the side of the miners."

"You be careful, Luke," Wright said soberly. "The mine owners won't cave in all that fast, the way I see it. They might try some kind of retaliation and you're as likely as not to be one of the targets of any retaliation if it comes since you're hell-bent on being a rabble-rouser."

"I'll be keeping my head low and my hopes high, Bill. Thanks again for that editorial." Sutton handed the paper back to Wright and left the office.

As soon as he arrived home, he pulled a blank sheet of paper from his pocket and sat down at the kitchen table. He took the pencil from his pocket and wrote, "Dear Mrs. Penrose." The next words wouldn't come to him. How did you tell a woman that the sons she had sent to America with such hope were now beyond hope, were, in fact, dead and buried, both of them, side by side. Sutton put down the pencil. He braced his elbows on the table and dropped his head in his hands. He thought of words, of phrases, none of them quite right, all of them inadequate to convey the message he wanted to deliver.

More than an hour later, he had finally written the letter. It was a short one, but one in which he told Mrs. Penrose he had known Jack and, through him, Richie. He wrote that he shared her hurt because, just as she had lost two sons, he had lost one very good friend. He ended the letter by saying he was sorry for her trouble and expressing the wish that he was more clever with words so that he could tell her how he truly felt. He signed it, folded the paper, and then rummaged through Penrose's satchel until he found the scrap of paper with Mrs. Penrose's address on it. He took a blank envelope from a pack which Penrose had bound together with a length of string, addressed it, and then left the house and went to the post office to mail the letter.

When he returned home, he realized he had not eaten all day and set about frying salt pork and boiling beans.

He was eating the meal he had prepared when a knock sounded on the door. Bob Danvers, he thought, rising.

But, when he opened the door, he found Opal Harding standing outside. "Opal, what—"

She brushed past him, closed the door behind her, and flattened her back against it. "Luke," she began breathlessly, "you've got to get away from here."

"What's wrong, Opal? You look like you've seen a ghost and have been running from it ever since."

"I heard him talking. Manning sent a man from the mine with a message. He's sending men to— Luke, you've got to leave. You've got to go away. Right away. Now!"

Sutton gripped her arms and realized that she was trembling. "Take it easy now. I'm not sure I follow you. You're saying the mine superintendent's sending some men—where?"

She shook her head violently. "No. I'm sorry, I'm not making myself clear. My husband received a message about you from Manning. He knows that you persuaded the men to go out on strike. Roy has hired some of his bullyboys—the ones I know he uses on occasion to perform less than savory tasks —to come here and—he didn't actually say it, but I don't think Roy would care if they killed you!"

"What exactly did he tell them to do to me?"

"Teach you a lesson. Those were his words. I was there. He didn't know that you and I had met. Where are you going?"

Sutton didn't answer her as he opened a cabinet that stood

against the wall and reached inside it. He remained silent as he strapped his cartridge belt around his hips and then slid his Russian Model .44 caliber Smith & Wesson from its holster, checked its cylinder, and then returned it to his holster.

"What are you going to do?" Opal asked, her eyes on the gun hanging low on Sutton's right hip. "You're not going to—" Her eyes rose and met his.

"How many men's your husband sending out after me?"

"I don't know. More than one. I don't know exactly how many. Luke, why don't you just go away? Anywhere. To Carson City. Just until things settle down."

"For one thing, there's no telling how long it'll take for things to settle down," Sutton said thoughtfully, his gray eyes on Opal. "For another, your husband, if I read him right, isn't going to be satisfied until he gets me out of his way."

"But it's all so simple!" Opal protested. She crossed the room to stand in front of Sutton. She placed her hands on his shoulders and, looking up at him, said, "All you have to do is go away."

"Run?"

"It wouldn't be running. It would be—" she hesitated before finally concluding "—it would be more a matter of prudence."

"Opal, I guess I've never been what you could call a prudent man. I *know* I'm not a man to turn tail and run from a fight."

"But you might be killed!"

"I might be," Sutton admitted soberly. "But I'm a hard man to kill. Too mean, I guess." He offered Opal a small smile.

Her face remained tense, her features strained.

"Don't worry," he advised. "Maybe your husband's men won't be able to find me."

"They know you live here. One of them said he'd heard you were bunking with Jack Penrose."

Sutton's arms went around Opal's waist. He drew her closer to him. "I do thank you for coming here with your warning." He kissed her gently and was pleased to find that she responded readily to him, moving close to him so that her body pressed against his and her hands slid from his shoulders and encircled his body.

"I don't want thanks, Luke," she said later as their kiss ended. "I want you alive."

"Then you and me, we want pretty much the same thing. How long before your husband's men get here, do you figure?"

"I have no way of knowing. I do know however that he was very angry and he indicated that he wanted what he called 'this matter' attended to with—I'm quoting him again—'dispatch.'"

"You've got to get out of here, Opal. It wouldn't do for those men to pop in here and spot you with me. It wouldn't look good. Worse, it could get you in a lot of trouble with your husband." He bent down and gently kissed the purple bruise beneath her eye.

"I'm not afraid," she said bravely but her quavering voice betrayed her.

"Go on now, Opal. Get out of here. Try to make sure nobody sees you leave."

"You won't go away?"

Sutton shook his head.

Opal sighed and then she embraced him fiercely and kissed him just as fiercely.

Behind her, the door to the house was suddenly booted open and two men with drawn guns stormed into the room.

Opal turned quickly and stood with her back against Sutton, trying to shield him from the pair of gunmen.

"Well, ain't it one real small world, Tulley?" said one of the two gunmen, grinning at Opal. "The boss's wife and the man we've come to see cozying up to one another. Now, don't that beat all?"

"I know somebody who's going to get beat once the boss finds out about this," Tulley said, his cold eyes on Opal. "You get my drift, Mercer?"

Mercer's grin widened. "Sutton, you toss that gun you're packing on the bunk over there."

"You, Mrs. Harding," Tulley said, gesturing with his revolver, "step away from Sutton else you're likely to get by accident some of what we came to deliver to him."

"The gun, Sutton," Mercer barked.

Sutton unholstered his Smith & Wesson and tossed it onto the bunk on the far side of the room. "Get out of here, Opal."

"How much is my husband paying you for—for this?" she asked Mercer and Tulley. "Whatever it is, I'll pay you more to leave Mr. Sutton alone."

"Mercer and me," Tulley said, "we operate on a strictly cash-and-carry basis. You got cash on you, Mrs. Harding?"

"No, but I—I can get it. I—"

"You move over to the other side of the room, Mrs. Harding," Mercer interrupted. "Hurry it up now."

"Let her go," Sutton said. "She's not part of this. It's me you want."

"You're right about that last part," Mercer snapped. "But you're dead wrong about the first part. It looks to me like Mrs. Harding's a very big part of this. Looks to me like after she heard us talking back at the house she lit out to come here and warn you about what we'd planned to do to you. I have a hunch her husband will want to hear all about her being here with you, Sutton. Now, Mrs. Harding, you move on over there like I told you."

As Opal crossed to the far side of the room, Mercer barked an order and Tulley positioned himself behind Sutton. He holstered his six-shooter and seized Sutton's arms, pinioning them behind Sutton's back.

Mercer also holstered his gun and then stepped closer to Sutton. He drew back his right fist and landed a right uppercut on Sutton's jaw which caused Sutton's head to snap backward. Mercer's next move, a hard right jab to Sutton's midsection, sent Sutton's head and shoulders bending toward Mercer who stepped back, raised both fists, and brought them down hard on the base of Sutton's skull.

"Stop it!" Opal cried. She ran to Mercer and seized his arm. He flung her aside and sent his right fist crashing into the side of Sutton's head. He used both fists then to pummel Sutton's body fiercely.

As Sutton gasped desperately for breath, Mercer finally relented and took a backward step. As he did so, Sutton braced himself against Tulley who was still gripping his arms. He brought both boots up off the floor and slammed them into Mercer's chest. As Mercer staggered backward, spluttering, Sutton doubled over, lifting Tulley's feet off the floor.

"Hey!" the surprised Tulley yelled.

Sutton went down on his knees, somersaulted, and came up straddling Tulley who had been thrown over his back to land with a thud on the wooden floor.

Opal cried out, her hands flying up to cover her mouth.

Sutton, alerted, saw Mercer make his move. He flattened himself against Tulley's supine body and Mercer's shot went harmlessly over him to lodge in the far wall.

Before Mercer could fire again, Sutton had Tulley's revolver out of its holster. He rose to his knees, fired once, missed the dodging Mercer, fired again, and dropped the man.

Tulley slammed a fist into Sutton's jaw and, as Sutton let out a cry of pain, Tulley tore his gun from Sutton's hand and shoved him aside.

"Luke!" Opal cried and knocked the gun from Tulley's hand.

Tulley scrambled along the floor toward it but Sutton, in one bound, reached the cot and his own .44.

Tulley reached his gun and got off a snapshot which went wild.

Sutton fired almost simultaneously.

His bullet entered Tulley's left cheek and tore out of the back of the man's skull, leaving a bloody hole behind it. Tulley flopped to the floor. His body shuddered. His fingers clawed at the wooden planking of the floor for a moment. Then they relaxed and went limp.

Sutton went over to Mercer and turned the man's body over with the toe of his boot.

Mercer's eyes were closed. His body remained motionless.

"Are they both—"

"Dead, looks like," Sutton answered Opal. He turned to her, holstering his gun. "It's time you went home."

"To my husband who sent these two men to kill you," Opal said, her voice grating in the room's stillness. "He won't have this incident to brag about the way he usually does because this time he came up against a man who was able to beat him at his own game."

"Harding's a braggart, is he?" Sutton inquired, not really interested in the answer but wanting to say something to help soften the sense of shock Opal was obviously still feeling.

"He likes to tell the story of how he got his start in Virginia City," she said, not looking at Sutton. Staring down at the two men on the floor, she continued, "He would cut up silver dollars and salt worthless claims with them and then sell those claims to men he still calls 'suckers.' Roy Harding built his present fortune on the backs of all the other men he cheated and brought to grief."

Sutton suddenly found himself listening to Opal with real interest.

"'Everybody did it in those days,' Roy likes to say, as if that's an excuse."

"Did he ever mention anybody by name—anybody he cheated by salting worthless claims?"

Opal, as if awakening from a bad dream, turned, frowning, toward Sutton. "No, I don't think so. I don't recall—wait, yes, I do recall a name. Loft. Lester Loft. No, that's not right." Her frown deepened. "Croft! That's the name. Lester Croft. Roy likes to laugh about the fact that Croft thought he was going to be a rich man and now he's nothing but a swamper in Carson City's Silver Saloon. Why do you ask, Luke?"

Sutton, ignoring her question, said, "Go home, Opal." He put out one rough hand and gently touched her cheek. "Thanks for coming here to warn me. I appreciate it."

"You aren't going to risk staying here now, are you?"

"Nope. I'm not. There's no use tempting fate to try to take me down a second time. I've got a friend who'll probably put me up. His name's Kee Chin. Him and his granddaughter, they live in a boardinghouse on Mount Davidson that caters to Chinese."

"You're going there now?"

"Nope, not right away. First off, I'm taking me a trip to Carson City tomorrow to have myself a talk with Lester Croft."

"Whatever for, Luke?"

"Well, I've got me a hopeful notion that Croft might be able to help me scald your husband's hide."

CHAPTER 8

The moment Sutton stepped off the train in Carson City the next morning, he headed directly for the Silver Saloon.

When he reached it, he went through the batwings and directly up to the bar. He beckoned to the bar dog.

"What'll you have, mister?" the man asked him.

"Information. About a man who works for you. Lester Croft."

The bar dog's eyebrows rose and his mouth opened, his lips forming a pink oval. "Now, why would you—anybody, for that matter—want information about old Lester?"

"I said I wanted information, not that I came here to give it to you or anybody else."

The bar dog caught the glint in Sutton's smoky eyes. His lips closed and his eyebrows descended. "Lester lives in a shack out back. He's probably out there now."

Sutton left the saloon and made his way around the building. In the rear, he spotted the plank building with the tar-paper roof which certainly qualified, he thought, as a shack. He went up to it and was about to knock when the door, which hung on leather hinges, swung open. He stepped quickly to one side to avoid a viscous stream of brownish liquid that came shooting out of the doorway.

"Croft," he said to the man standing just inside the shack who was staring at him in surprise and holding the brass spittoon he had just emptied. "Want to have a word or two with you."

"Don't know you, mister. Never saw you before in my life." Croft started to close the door.

Sutton thrust a boot out and kicked the door wide open, his eyes riveted on the man he thought to be beyond fifty and maybe beyond a whole lot more than that, judging by his bleary eyes and the broken veins visible in his nose.

"You got no call to go acting like that. I'm a peaceable man. I don't bother folks. I try to keep out of their way so's they don't bother me. What for are you raising a ruckus with old Lester?"

"I'm fixing to raise no ruckus with you, Croft. I told you. I just want to talk to you."

"What about?"

"Let's go inside." Sutton shouldered his way past Croft into the one-room shack which was, he noticed immediately, not only incredibly filthy but decidedly malodorous.

A cluster of spittoons sat on the dirt floor. Dirty rags lay beside them. A canister of polish sat in the midst of the rags.

Croft sat down on the floor beside the spittoons and used a dirty rag to wipe out the interior of the one he held in his hands. "You want to talk, mister, talk."

"I heard you bought a worthless mining claim some time back in Virginia City. That true?"

Croft squinted up at Sutton. "How'd you find out about that? That was all of two years ago or more. Who told you?"

"Doesn't matter much who told me. Is what I was told the truth?"

Croft, instead of replying, got to his feet and went to a shelf that was nailed to one wall, took a bottle of Rosebud from it, opened it, and drank from it. He licked his lips and then resumed his seat on the floor.

"Well, Croft?" Sutton prompted.

"I'll allow that what you say is true." He took another swallow of whiskey from the bottle. "I was taken, no two ways about that. Damn fool that I was."

"What happened?"

"I owned a feed store in St. Louis some years back, but I got the notion I'd like to be a rich a man so I picked up me and my missus and we came to Virginia City after selling our house and my business. Had more'n ten thousand dollars in my pocket in those days. Went looking for a silver mine to buy. Oh, I was cocky back then, I can tell you. I was going to be another old man Hearst, I was."

"Go on."

"Met me a man who said he'd heard I was interested in mining property. I remember it like it was yesterday. Met him in a Gold Hill saloon across the ridge from Virginia City. Well, sir, he took me out the very next day and showed me a shaft he'd sunk—or said he'd sunk. Wasn't much of one. Short, it was. Said it was a rich one and he let me climb down and have myself an on-the-spot look-see."

"You found ore?"

"Found nuggets of silver all mixed up with barren rock down there and—"

"Wait a minute. Silver seldom shows up in nugget form."

Croft laughed, a cackling sound, and then drowned his laughter by drinking from his bottle. He held it out to Sutton. "Have a drink? It's good whiskey. I don't get paid in cash. I get whiskey, this place to live in, some vittles."

"No thanks."

"Suit yourself. Well, the long and the short of it is, I bought the mine."

"Didn't you have the nuggets you found assayed first?"

Croft shook his head. "I told you I was a damn fool. I was advised by the seller to keep the whole thing under my hat so nobody'd jump my claim. I signed some papers and turned over almost six thousand dollars to become owner of what turned out to be a salted mine—one that wasn't worth the powder to blow it up. Found that out when I finally did take some of those nuggets in to the assay office. Oh, they were silver alright. They'd been cut from silver half dollars, pounded into lumps, blackened a bit, and then thrown down the shaft. The assayer, he laughed till he about burst when he showed me a nugget on which you could make out the letters 'of Ameri . . .'

"The missus never let me hear the end of it. She said I was a fool and I guess she was right. She just never stopped saying it, not even when she took to what turned out to be her deathbed less than a year later. I like to claim she ruined me, the way she made me feel worse than a fool, and a whole lot less than a man. It took the starch right out of me. Now—well, you can see what I've come down to. But it wasn't the fault of my missus. I just lost my nerve after I lost all that money. Went to pieces slow but sure." Croft put down the bottle and poured polish from the canister on the spittoon. He picked up another cloth and began to burnish it.

Sutton took a step toward him.

Croft pointed. "Your boots sure are dusty." He looked up at Sutton. "I earn a little spare change in the saloon by polishing fellows' boots. I could do a real fine job on yours for you. Make 'em glisten real good. Two bits."

Sutton shook his head.

"Ten cents?"

"You never brought charges against the man who sold you the claim, Croft?"

Croft shook his head, put down the spittoon he had been polishing, and drank more Rosebud. "Maybe I should have, but lawyers cost money then as now and I had little of that left after the fiasco I got myself caught up in. Oh, I hope he burns in hellfire for what he did to me. And I want to be sitting right there in a ringside seat to watch Adam Foss barbecue."

Sutton's mind suddenly reeled. He stared through narrowed eyes at Croft who went on busily polishing his spittoon. "Did you—" he began but his voice gave out on him. "Did you," he tried again, "mean to say that *Adam Foss* sold you that worthless claim?"

"I did." Croft, when Sutton said nothing more, looked up. "What's wrong, mister? You look awful pale and sweaty all of a sudden. You sick or something?"

Sutton swallowed hard. "I was told a man by the name of Roy Harding sold you that claim."

"You were told wrong, mister."

"It wasn't Harding?"

"Don't know nobody by that name so how could it have been him?"

"You remember what Foss looked like?"

"I'll never forget him. Short as a tallow barrel. He wore a beard that looked like rats had been nesting in it. You know this man Foss?"

"I know him. I remember him as being skinny—bones sticking out all over his body."

"That's right. He was a fidgety kind of customer too."

Sutton remembered the night it had all begun. He remembered Foss and the way the man's eyes had constantly darted from person to person, from place to place. He remembered the habit Foss had had of shifting his weight from one foot to the other. He described those characteristics to Croft.

"You have him pegged alright. That's Foss, sure enough." Croft put down the spittoon he had polished and picked up another one. "Where'd you get the notion that it was Harding who sold me that claim?"

"There's a man named Roy Harding in Virginia City and I was told—by someone I believe—that it was him who sold you that claim. But you say it was Foss, not Harding. Which leaves me with only one conclusion to jump to."

"That Foss changed his name to Harding somewhere along the line," Croft interjected.

"That's the size of it."

"Makes sense, it does. Foss dropped clean out of sight soon after he duped me and a few others. Then I came over here. Looks like Foss showed up again wearing a brand-new monicker."

"I've been thinking, maybe you could get him into court for cheating you." Sutton told Croft about what was happening in Virginia City's mines and about the part that Foss, alias Roy Harding, had in it.

Croft held up a hand and shook his head. "You'll have to find yourself somebody else to go after Foss for you. Ain't nobody'd pay any attention to an old rumpot like me, were I to take the witness stand. Besides, that's all water under the dam now. All I want now is to try to forget about it. This helps." He held up the bottle of Rosebud and then drank heartily from it.

"Sorry to have bothered you." Sutton started for the door.

"Weren't no bother. I wish you good luck with Foss. Nothing'd make me happier than to see him get as good as he gave to suckers like me. I'll think some more on what you suggested. Maybe if I ever get up to Virginia City again and I happen to be sober at the time I'll do just what you want. Bring charges against Foss."

Sutton started for the door, thinking that it didn't matter now. If Croft ever did try to bring charges against Foss, he'd find himself suing a corpse.

"Say," Croft called out. "You sure you don't want me to shine those boots of yours for you? For just five cents?"

Sutton shook his head and went through the door, heading for the train depot. As he strode purposefully along the streets of Carson City, the pity he had been feeling for Croft was gradually replaced by the familiar fire of his hatred for Foss. It burned low but bright within him.

In the distance, he saw the boardinghouse in which he had so recently lived. He thought of Mrs. Reardon and the kindnesses she had shown him. He thought of Eileen Dugan, of her beauty, of the feel of her soft skin. He wanted to detour and visit them both. But the fire within him burned on, hot and demanding, and he continued walking in the direction in which he was headed, silently cursing Foss who, though distant, tugged and tore at his life until it had no direction of its own, only one dictated by the fact that Foss was still alive, leaving Sutton himself unavenged.

Three men dead, he thought. Maybe, for another man, that'd be enough. But it's not for me. I'll get you, Foss, he silently vowed. I'm on my way to you, Foss. It'll be good to see you again, he thought wryly. Real good. Fine, in fact.

Sutton leaped from the train before it had pulled to a halt and loped out of the depot. It didn't take him long to reach the office of the *Territorial Enterprise* where he found Wright.

"What's been going on, Bill?" he asked.

"That's some general question, Luke," Wright responded, his eyes twinkling. "You mean what's been going on with the Ladies' Social Circle of Virginia City?"

"You know what I mean, Bill. What about mines other than the High Stakes? Did their men go out too?"

"It's a complete close-down or the very next thing to it," Wright replied. "There are, however, a few holdouts." Wright named three mines. "But they're working on just a single shift and without a full work force. Why did you have to leave town?"

"If I tell you, you'll go printing all about it in your newspaper and then I'll really be in trouble."

"Seriously, Luke. Was something wrong? *Is* something wrong? I note that you've taken to wearing a gun."

Sutton told Wright that Harding's men had attacked him but not that Harding was, in reality, Adam Foss.

"You could move in with me until things settle down," Wright suggested. "Like you just said, you can't risk going back to Penrose's place."

"I'm much obliged for the offer, Bill. I appreciate it. But I've got someplace in mind. Tell you what, though. If the place I've got in mind doesn't pan out, well, can I consider your generous offer still open?"

"Of course you can."

"Good." Sutton turned and headed for the door.

"Luke!"

Sutton turned and Wright said, "You be careful, hear?"

Sutton grinned and said, "I'll be as careful as a broody hen hatching eggs. How's that?"

When Wright returned his grin, Sutton left the office and started out for the boardinghouse where Kee Chin and Mei-ling were staying. Once safely there, he promised himself, he'd get right to work on planning the best way to go about getting Foss.

He couldn't help noticing, as he walked through the town, the many solemn faces of the people he passed in the streets. He noticed too that the town seemed unusually quiet.

Things're coming to a head, he thought. You can sense the strain in the air. It's like the dead dry stillness that settles in a place just before a storm strikes.

He was still some distance away from the boardinghouse when he heard an explosion in the distance. It was followed by the indecipherable shouts of men and then, quickly, by a second explosion.

He turned and sprinted toward the shouting in the distance, making his way up the slope of Mount Davidson, dodging the people in the streets, aware that other men were also running in the same direction, all of them as grim-faced and as silent as he himself was.

"The High Stakes!" a man behind Sutton shouted.

Sutton realized the man was right. He could see smoke rising above the mine's buildings not far ahead of him. He increased his pace and came running out into the sprawling area of buildings, ore carts, mule barns, the hoisting works, and the ore-crushing building.

His eyes took in the cluster of men who were standing atop filled ore carts and bending down to other men below them who passed up bundles, each of which contained five sticks of dynamite which were bound together and neatly fitted with percussion caps.

He saw other men engaged in brutal hand-to-hand combat in front of the ore-crushing building.

Sutton grabbed a man who was racing past him and spun him around. "What's going on here?" he yelled above the noise of the battling men and the occasional explosions which resulted from hurled bundles of dynamite.

"Scabs!" the man screamed, his face contorted with fury. "Harding's gone and rounded up the rabble and put them to working his mine. We're trying to stop them. We're *going* to stop them!" The man ripped himself free of Sutton and ran down into the midst of the battling men.

Sutton ran toward the ore carts and, when he reached the nearest one, he climbed up on it. He seized the dynamite in the hand of the man nearest to him and, holding the startled man away from him with his left hand, he used his teeth to rip out the burning fuse and then hurled the sticks of dynamite to the ground.

"What're you doing?" the man shrieked, breaking away from Sutton. "You started all this and now you're trying to stop it. You lost your mind?"

"This is not the way to win what you men want!" Sutton bellowed. "Not by fighting or maybe killing."

"What do you want us to do? Escort those scabs right on into the hoisting works? Pack their dinner pails for them?"

"Set up a string of men around the hoisting works to keep Harding's men from getting inside."

"We tried that! It didn't work. But *this* will!" The man reached down and received another five-stick bundle of dynamite from an upthrust hand. "We'll blow the whole place to kingdom come. Those scabs won't have a place to work by the time we're finished here."

"Neither will you!" Sutton yelled, exasperated.

As the man lit the fuse on the bundle of dynamite he was holding, Sutton knocked it from his hand. It struck the ore piled in the cart and bounced down to the ground.

"Get him!" the man yelled, pointing at Sutton.

Sutton suddenly felt himself seized from behind. He tried to turn but something hard—a gun butt, he realized—struck him just above his right ear. The explosion in his skull was matched by another one which was the result of a thrown bundle of dynamite. It blew open the door of the hoisting works.

He finally managed to turn toward his attacker. He landed a swift uppercut. But, before he could throw another punch, his assailant kicked him and he felt himself falling. He hit the edge of the ore cart, bounced off it, and fell to the ground.

He lay there a moment, groggy, and then he started to get shakily to his feet. He was on his knees when the dynamite that he had knocked from the man's hand earlier exploded on the opposite side of the cart.

The two men on top of the ore cart leaped from it as the cart rose into the air and then came crashing down. It then started to tilt dangerously to one side.

Sutton, as it began to tilt, summoned his energies and desperately threw himself to one side.

He almost made it.

But the ore cart, as it toppled, spilled its contents. One huge chunk of ore came crashing down to strike the side of Sutton's head, bringing with it a starless night and a wild wind which swept him into unconsciousness.

Sutton slowly returned to consciousness, aware of shouts punctuated by distant explosions.

He opened his eyes to a blurred world. He closed them tightly and then opened them again, shaking his head in an effort to bring his vision into focus.

He was lying face down on the ground and, as he tried to rise, pain shot through his skull, reminding him of what had happened—how long ago? It might have been a few seconds ago, as far as he knew. Or a lifetime.

Fist fights still raged in the distance. Smoke still dirtied the surrounding air. Metal clanged harshly against metal and Sutton made out two men, both half hidden in a dense cloud of smoke which was billowing up from an unseen source, battling each other, one wielding a crowbar, the other a pickaxe.

Fools, he thought, pushing himself up onto his hands and knees. He knelt on the ground a moment, his head hanging down, to steady himself. Drops of bright red blood from his scalp wound dripped down into the dust.

Those men are smart enough to know what they want, he thought. But they're not smart enough to know the best way to go about getting it. He took a deep breath and, gripping the edge of the overturned ore cart with both hands, he hauled himself erect. He stood there a moment, leaning against the cart, his breathing shallow, before taking his first unsteady step. And then another. A third. He swayed and almost lost his balance but he kept on walking.

He concentrated on putting one foot in front of the other. Kee Chin, he thought. I'll get to his place, he told himself. All I got to do is keep going, one step at a time, and forget about the way my head hurts.

The ground shifted beneath his boots. He swayed. But he didn't fall. He stood still for a moment until the ground under him solidified and then he walked slowly and unsteadily on.

By the time he reached Chin's boardinghouse, the sun above him seemed to have dimmed and was threatening to wink out at any moment. He knocked on the door and when it was opened by a tiny Chinese woman of indeterminate age he muttered, "Kee Chin."

The woman gasped and stepped backward.

Sutton moved past her, made a grab for the staircase's railing, and then began climbing the stairs, taking one step at a time. Once on the second-floor landing, he braced himself against the wall and made his way to Chin's door.

He didn't bother to knock. He turned the porcelain knob of the door handle and, as the door opened, he stumbled into the room and fell to his knees.

"Luke!"

He heard Chin's voice coming to him from a great distance and he tried to speak but found that he couldn't utter any words.

He heard someone speaking a language he didn't understand. He felt someone's hands under his armpits. He seemed to be rising toward the ceiling which wavered indistinctly above him. Then he felt himself settling down on something soft.

Someone sighed.

He realized dimly that it was he who had sighed.

Night suddenly shrouded him.

When the deep night died sometime later, he realized that he had passed out again. He looked around.

Mei-ling.

He tried to smile at her and she bent, concern etched on her delicate features, toward him. "No," she said, "don't try to get up. Lie still."

" . . . no place else . . . to go," he managed to murmur. "Sorry."

"Quiet!" she said firmly and sat down in a chair beside the bed.

"Fracas," he said. Then, after carefully lining up the words in his mind, he added, "Got caught right in the middle of it."

Mei-ling frowned.

"How long . . ." It was too much of an effort to finish the question he had started. He stared dully at Mei-ling.

"You came here a little more than an hour ago. I washed your wound and put on a linen bandage."

Sutton slowly raised his right hand and felt the wad of cloth covering his scalp wound and the narrow band of cloth that circled his head to hold the bandage in place. "Much obliged."

"He's awake," Mei-ling said and Sutton saw the face of Kee Chin appear on the opposite side of the bed. It seemed to hang suspended there as the elderly man looked worriedly down at him.

"Got something to tell you, Chin."

"Not now, Luke. You will be safe here."

"Had no other place to go to," Sutton murmured.

"We are glad you came," Mei-ling said. "You have given us the opportunity to repay the debt we owe you."

"Debt?"

Chin smiled. "You remember telling me about my stock, about it being of no value? About what Harding was doing, buying up stock in his High Stakes Mine?"

Sutton nodded.

"I am, thanks to you, Luke, a rich man. Modestly so, but still rich."

Sutton's eyes held a question.

Chin answered it by saying, "The High Stakes stock has been rising steadily. I have a profit—on paper—of almost seven thousand dollars."

"Sell the stock," Sutton said sharply. "Sell it now. Today."

"But it keeps rising," Chin protested. "By tomorrow it will be worth—"

"Sell it!" Sutton repeated. "News of the discovery of that new ore vein at the High Stakes'll spread far and wide real soon. Foss—I mean Harding'll be dumping his holdings any minute now and the stock will fall fast."

Chin looked across the bed at Mei-ling.

"Do what Luke suggests, Grandfather."

Chin nodded.

Sutton closed his eyes, weariness washing over him.

The sudden knock on the door sounded like thunder to him. His eyes flicked open. He watched Mei-ling walk to the door and open it. He saw her stumble backward into the room.

"Let's go, Sutton!"

The man who had barked the order, the man who had rudely thrust Mei-ling aside as he entered the room, had a Colt .45 in his hand and a badge pinned to his vest.

Mei-ling said something to Kee Chin in Chinese. The old man answered her. Neither of them moved. Then both of them turned to stare at Sutton as he slowly began to rise from the bed.

"What's the charge, Sheriff?" he asked as his boots touched the floor.

"Murder," the sheriff replied bluntly. "Found out you're wanted down in Texas for the murder of your brother."

Sutton had been about to stand but, as the sheriff's words and what he believed they meant racketed in his mind, his body stiffened. "Harding told you about that?"

"How'd you know—"

"How'd you know I was here?"

"Never mind how I knew. What's important is I've found you. Now get yourself up on your feet, Sutton. We're getting out of here, you and me."

Sutton got to his feet, aware of the shocked expressions on the faces of Kee Chin and Mei-ling. He slowly crossed the room.

"Hold it," ordered the sheriff. He unbuckled Sutton's gunbelt and draped it over his shoulder before prodding Sutton with his gun barrel.

Sutton walked out into the hall, thinking that he knew the answer to the question he had asked the sheriff.

There was only one way the sheriff could have known that he might be at Kee Chin's because there was only one person he had told he was going there.

That person's name was Opal Harding.

CHAPTER 9

On the morning of the day following his arrest, Sutton had a
visitor.

Mei-ling, followed by the sheriff, came through the door
which separated the jail cells from the sheriff's front office.
She stood, hands folded, in front of the bars, her eyes on Sutton as he got up from his bunk and crossed his cell to greet
her.

"Didn't expect to see you here, Mei-ling."

Her eyes dropped. "I did not expect to come here."

The sheriff stood with folded arms just inside the cell area, leaning indolently against the door frame.

"You and your granddaddy doing alright?"

Mei-ling was silent for a moment and then, ignoring Sutton's question, she asked one of her own. "Did you do it?"

Sutton was not surprised by the question. In fact, he had been expecting it, had assumed that it might be the reason why Mei-ling had visited him—to ask that very question.

"No," he answered, "I didn't kill my brother."

She looked up at him. "But the sheriff said—"

"He's got it all wrong. I'll tell you what happened." Sutton gripped the bars with both hands. "One night more'n three years ago, four men showed up at the homeplace I shared with my younger brother, Dan. They . . ."

Mei-ling listened without interrupting as Sutton recounted all that had happened that night so long ago, and, in retelling it, he found himself reliving the events of that ugly night which had so radically altered his life and ended his brother's. As he spoke, his words began to rush from him. He told Mei-ling about the map which, it had been claimed, pinpointed the location of the lost San Saba Mine. He talked of the fight that had occurred, of the gunplay and its result: his trial for murder.

When he had finished his account, he leaned his forehead against the cold iron of the bars, feeling drained and empty of all emotion, except for the lust for vengeance against Adam Foss which was still a fiery fever burning within him.

"I believe you," Mei-ling said simply and Sutton raised his head.

"Grandfather and I are returning to San Francisco on the stage tomorrow," she said.

"Hope you'll have a good trip. Tell your granddaddy I said good-bye."

"I have a message for you, Luke."

"From him?"

Mei-ling shook her head and took a step closer to the bars. She glanced at the sheriff who was lighting a cigar and then, turning to Sutton, she whispered, "Mrs. Harding asked me to tell you that she is sorry she told her husband that you might be visiting us."

Sutton snorted his disdain. "Lot of good her being sorry will do me now." And then, "She came to see you?"

"Yes. She said she did not dare come here because if she did and her husband found out about it he would beat her again."

"He beat her?"

"She was badly bruised. Her wrist was sprained and in a sling. She said he found out that she had been to visit you before you came to us."

"Now, how could he find out about that?"

"A man—a man named Mercer, Mrs. Harding said—told her husband she had been to see you."

Sutton swore. "I thought I'd killed Mercer."

"Mrs. Harding said she also thought you had done so. She said you did kill the other man who was with him."

"If she comes to see you again, Mei-ling, you tell her to stay away. Tell her don't worry about me. I'll make out. Tell her she's got to think about herself—about her own safety."

"She will not come again, she said. And we are leaving Virginia City tomorrow, Grandfather and me."

"Good on both scores. You could get the pair of you in trouble too if you get mixed up with me."

The sheriff, still lounging in the doorway and smoking, said, "Time's up, lady."

"I would very much like to kiss you good-bye, Luke."

As Mei-ling stepped closer to the bars, Sutton leaned down. As their lips met, he felt her thrust something into his hand.

Their lips parted and she whispered, "From Mrs. Harding."

Sutton, before Mei-ling moved away from the bars, pocketed the derringer she had given him. "Thanks," he said. "Thanks a whole lot."

"When you get out of here, do you have a place to go?" Mei-ling asked anxiously.

"I'll hole up with a friend of mine, Bill Wright. He runs a newspaper, the *Territorial Enterprise*, here in town."

"Thank you for everything you have done for Grandfather and me." Mei-ling quickly kissed Sutton a second time and then hurried away from the bars, past the sheriff, and out into the office.

The sheriff closed the door behind her, leaving Sutton alone in his cell with his racing thoughts—and the derringer Opal had smuggled to him by way of Mei-ling.

Sutton returned to his bunk and sat down upon it. Keeping one eye on the door leading to the sheriff's office, he took the derringer from the pocket of his jeans and examined it. It was, he saw, a .41 caliber single-shot Colt. It had a two-and-one-half-inch barrel with a snap latch on which the name "Colt" appeared and a spring ejector.

He hefted the gun, noting its bird's head walnut grips and nickel-plated brass frame. Its total length of four and one half inches didn't reach from Sutton's wrist to the tips of his fingers. He knew it had no range to speak of. Would it do the job he had in mind for it? It would have to.

He gripped the gun, his index finger resting lightly on its spur trigger. Then he checked to see if the gun was loaded by swinging the barrel to the right. It was loaded. He returned the barrel to its former position, pocketed the gun, and then leaned back against the stone wall, his eyes on the door that led to the sheriff's office. He willed it to move, to open.

Twenty minutes later, when it did open, he rose from his bunk and crossed the cell to grip the bars with both hands.

"That Texas lawman you told me you sent for, did he get here yet, Sheriff?"

"How could he? He can't fly."

"When do you expect he will get here?"

"In a week, maybe two. Meanwhile, you just relax and enjoy Virginia City's hospitality." The sheriff tossed the wet mop he had been carrying toward a corner of the room. It fell short and landed in front of Sutton's cell.

"I'd be obliged, Sheriff, if you'd get that mop out of there. It sure does stink something fierce."

"I take it you've got delicate sensibilities, Sutton."

Move, Sutton thought, his cold eyes on the sheriff.

The sheriff came toward the cell and Sutton readied himself but, before he could make his move, the sheriff gave the mop a kick that sent it clattering along the wooden floor and out of sight.

Before it had come to rest, the sheriff was on his way back toward the open door.

"Sheriff!"

When the man turned back to look back at him, Sutton smiled and said, "You wouldn't happen to have the makings on you, would you now?"

"You want waiting on hand and foot, Sutton," the sheriff muttered as he turned and started through the doorway.

"Please, Sheriff," Sutton said, his tone close to a whine. "I want a smoke and I'm all out of both papers and tobacco. I hate to beg but I do need a smoke."

"You hate to beg, do you?" the sheriff said as he turned again to face Sutton. "What would you say if I said I enjoy hearing a man like you beg?" He pulled a cloth sack of Bull Durham from his shirt pocket and held it out at arm's length. "Well, Sutton, just how bad do you want to smoke?"

"Please," Sutton said, his eyes on the sack in the sheriff's hand. He thrust his left hand through the bars.

"You're *begging* me for a smoke, Sutton?"

Sutton dropped his eyes. "I'm begging you, Sheriff."

The sheriff's laughter erupted from his lips. He came toward Sutton, still laughing, and, as Sutton made a grab for the sack, he jerked it out of his reach.

"You hard cases are all alike, Sutton. All show and no sand when things go against you. Here!" He thrust the sack at Sutton.

But Sutton, instead of taking it, seized the sheriff's wrist that held it. His right hand came up and in it was the .41 he had pulled from his pocket. He jerked his left arm and the sheriff slammed up against the bars, his face only inches away from Sutton's.

Sutton placed the barrel of the derringer against the lawman's throat. "I'll be doing without that smoke. *You'll* be getting the key to this cell out of your pocket and unlocking this door."

"You've played the wrong card, Sutton. The key's out in my office."

Sutton's stern expression didn't change. He released the sheriff's wrist and his left hand cupped the back of the sheriff's neck. "I saw you pocket that key after you locked me up yesterday. I saw you take the same key out of your pocket this morning to let that drunk out of this cell and after you'd locked this door again that key went back into your pocket."

"I swear I don't have it. You can search me."

"I can't search you and you know I can't. If I let go my grip on your neck you'll be out of range of this gambler's gun I've got before rain can soak through unpainted canvas. And speaking of gambling, I'm gambling you've got the key in your pocket. You say it's out there in your office. I'm going to count to three. If you haven't unlocked this cell door by then, you're a dead man and I won't be a whole lot worse off than I am right this minute. *One!*"

"You wouldn't—"

"*Two!*"

"Don't shoot, Sutton!"

Sutton kept his grip on the sheriff's neck as the man fumbled about in his pants pocket and came up with the key.

"I got it. See? Here it is—the key."

"Use it!"

When the cell door had been unlocked, Sutton booted it open, sending the sheriff stumbling backward. He sprang forward and ripped the man's gun from its holster. "Now, we're going out into your office and you're going to give me back my gun."

"Sure, Sutton. You want your gun—you got it."

A moment later, Sutton, in the outer office, thrust the .41 into his waistband and placed the sheriff's revolver on the desk. When the sheriff looked down at his gun, Sutton said, "Don't make a try for it."

The sheriff looked up at Sutton and dumbly shook his head as Sutton strapped on his cartridge belt.

"The cell—*you're* going in it now." Sutton marched the sheriff back through the door and into the cell. "I'll leave your gun out there on the desk."

The sheriff started to say something but, before he could get his words out, Sutton swiftly holstered his .44 and swung. His fist connected with the lawman's jaw, toppling him onto the bunk that had so recently been his own.

He seized the sheriff's shirt and ripped a piece from it as the sheriff lay limply, his eyes closed, on the bunk.

He tore a thin strip from the piece of cloth in his hand and then stuffed the rest of it into the sheriff's mouth. He tied the remaining strip around the sheriff's head to hold the gag in place and knotted it tightly. Then he left the cell and slammed the door behind him. He locked it and made his way out into the office where he threw the key onto the desk to lie beside the sheriff's revolver.

He went to the door, looked through its window, and then, pulling his hat down low on his forehead, went outside and began moving fast up the boardwalk to set into motion the plan he had conceived which would, he believed, bring him to the end of the long trail he had been following, the trail that would end soon when he once again came face to face with Foss.

He went directly to Wright's office and, as he entered it, he found Wright alone.

"Luke! Where have you been?"

"In jail," Sutton replied and then told Wright what had recently happened.

"That's absolutely astonishing!" Wright exclaimed when Sutton finished speaking. "You say that Roy Harding is really Adam Foss? Foss!" Wright repeated excitedly. "That's the man you asked me about the day we first met, isn't it?"

"It is. And, like I just told you, he's one of four men who shot me and killed my brother."

Wright, clearly amazed, sat down in a chair and stared speechlessly up at Sutton who said, "I'm going gunning for Foss as soon as it gets dark. I came here, Bill, to ask you if you'd let me hide out here till then."

"Luke, why don't you go to the sheriff about Foss and let him handle the matter?"

"Because the law's been of no help to me in this," Sutton answered stonily. "It's been a hindrance from the start, as a matter of fact. It's the law that put me in jail, claiming I killed my brother, and it was the law that was all set to slip a noose around my neck. No, this is a score I'm going to settle on my own."

"Tonight then promises to be a wild one in Virginia City," Wright commented in a low tone. "You, I gather, are thinking about committing murder and the miners, if my information is correct, and I believe it is, are planning violence against— did you know, Luke, that the state militia has been called in?"

"I didn't know."

"Dave Honeywell telegraphed the governor for troops to

protect the men the mine owners hired to work the mines during the strike. But I talked to Honeywell about the matter and it was apparent that he did what he did with great reluctance because he felt, he said, that the presence of the militiamen would only aggravate an already potentially explosive situation. He admitted to me when I questioned him that it was Harding—Foss—who wanted the troops brought here. He put a lot of pressure on Honeywell and the other members of the Mine Owners' Association." Wright hesitated, cleared his throat, and then continued, "I thought you were trying to work things out between the owners and the miners, Luke."

"I was. But now I've got something more important to take care of."

"Foss?"

"Foss. Now, Bill, where can I hole up?"

"In the pressroom."

"Anyone back there?"

"No, not now." Wright led Sutton into the rear room where the press was housed and then to a smaller room that opened off it. "We store our paper in here. It's not deluxe accommodations as you can see but—"

"It'll do fine, Bill. Thanks. Close the door when you go out."

Wright did and Sutton climbed up on a wired bale of paper and lay down upon it, his back resting against it, one ankle propped on a crooked knee. He placed his hat over his face, folded his arms across his chest, and waited for sleep to come to him.

It didn't.

He was still wide awake when the door opened. He sat up quickly, reaching for his .44.

"It's me, Luke," Wright said hastily. "Take it easy. There's someone in the outer office who wants to see you."

"You said I was here?"

"No. But I asked her to wait a moment and came back here to find out if you wanted to see her."

"Her?"

"A Chinese woman who said her name was Mei-ling."

"I'll see her. Bring her back here, will you, Bill?" Sutton followed Wright out into the pressroom.

A moment later, Mei-ling came running into it with Wright following her.

"Luke! Grandfather—he's—he needs help. Will you help him, Luke?"

"Slow down some, Mei-ling. What kind of trouble's your granddaddy in?"

"When I got home after visiting you in jail, a man was there. I heard him asking Grandfather where you were. I ran away and went to the sheriff but he wasn't there. You weren't either. No one was. I remembered you said you would come to stay with Mr. Wright when you got out of jail so I came here. Luke, will you help Grandfather?"

"He's got no call to now," Mercer said.

Sutton's eyes flicked from Mei-ling to Mercer who was standing in the entrance to the pressroom, a revolver in his right hand. "I heard somebody moving about out in the hall back there in your boardinghouse, missy," Mercer said to Mei-ling, "and when I looked out, there you were and already on the run. I figured you might be on your way to Sutton here so I up and followed you and just take a look how wonderful everything's turned out."

"Get out of here!" Wright ordered but Mercer ignored him, his eyes on Sutton, his gun aimed at Sutton's chest.

"Luke, I'm sorry," Mei-ling breathed and then, her voice unsteady, turned to Mercer. "My grandfather—"

"He's fine, missy. Just scared some."

"How did you know I was out of jail, Mercer?" Sutton asked.

"The sheriff's deputy turned him loose and he sent word to Mr. Harding about how you escaped."

"It was your boss who put the law onto me, wasn't it?"

"Sure it was," Mercer admitted. "Mr. Harding, he had an old wanted poster that some Texas lawman put out on you and he handed it over to the sheriff."

"Just what are you intending to do!" Wright demanded angrily, addressing Mercer.

"Nothing much. Just march this murderer back to the jail and see to it that he's locked up and kept where he belongs this time till the Texas law can get its hands on him again. Let's go, Sutton." Mercer gestured with his free hand in the direction of the door. "But first, you'd better drop that there gun you're wearing."

"Mei-ling—Wright," Sutton said. "You two go on out into the office and stay clear. Mercer there looks like he wouldn't mind shooting me if I gave him half a chance."

Wright glanced at Sutton. So did Mei-ling.

"Go on," he told them and they both began to move toward the door. "Let them pass, Mercer."

"You're not giving the orders around here, Sutton," Mercer barked. "I am. Now drop that gun of yours like I told you to do."

Sutton's right hand closed on the butt of his revolver. Suddenly, he sprang to the left.

Mercer let out a yelp and fired, his bullet missing Sutton and clanging off the metal press.

Sutton's .44 cleared leather and, before Mercer could make another move, he fired. The bullet went in under Mercer's gun hand and bore into his ribs on the right side.

Mercer, as he took the bullet, sidestepped because of its force and then, recovering himself, he turned and fired a second time at Sutton who dropped to one knee so that the bullet passed over his head.

Sutton fired again and then stood, feet firmly planted apart, smoke curling up from the barrel of his revolver, and watched Mercer bend forward, drop his gun, and then look up at Sutton in a kind of surprise that was tinged with terror.

Sutton said nothing.

Mei-ling stood, her eyes wide, staring in horror at Mercer as his body continued to fold in upon itself.

Wright's arm went around her shoulders as Mercer moaned and fell to the floor where he curled up in a quivering ball, his bloody fingers clawing at the holes in his body.

The silence was broken by Wright. "He's . . . is he dead, Luke?"

Sutton went over to Mercer and placed two fingers against the side of the man's neck. "He's dead," he said, straightening up. "Bill, I want you to do something for me—for Mei-ling and her granddaddy. Take her back to her boardinghouse.

"Mei-ling, you pack your things.

"Bill, when's the next stage due to head out for San Francisco?"

Wright pulled a watch from his vest pocket, snapped it open, looked at it, and said to Sutton, "In less than an hour."

"Bill, you take Mei-ling and her granddaddy to the stage and see that they get on it. It's not healthy here for either one of them on account of them being friends of mine."

Mei-ling ran to Sutton and threw her arms around him. "I'm sorry, Luke, that—I want to thank you but . . . Oh, there are so many things I want to say and I—"

"You cut out the crying now, Mei-ling. You've got yourself a job to do."

She looked up inquiringly at Sutton.

"You've got to look out for your granddaddy—and for yourself. You've got to see to it that the both of you get safely on that stage and started for home."

"Luke, if you're ever in San Francisco—" Mei-ling's tears began again.

Sutton gently wiped them away with an index finger and said, "I'll look you up. That's a promise."

"Bill," Sutton said as he holstered his .44, "you'd best hunt up the sheriff and tell him what happened here—how Mercer threw down on me—once you've gotten my friends on the stage."

Wright nodded and then he and Mei-ling were gone.

Sutton, after glancing again at Mercer's corpse, returned to the storage room and climbed up on the bale of newsprint. He thumbed a cartridge from one of his belt loops and inserted it in one of the two empty chambers in his gun's cylinder. He repeated the process, filling the other empty chamber, and then, his legs dangling over the edge of the bale, he idly turned the cylinder, thinking about which of the six cartridges would be the one to find its way from its chamber, down the barrel of the revolver, through the air, and into Foss's body.

Would there be more than one?

Sutton raised the gun and pointed it at the opposite wall. He caressed the trigger. In his mind, he eased it back, slowly, slowly . . .

Across the room from him Foss cringed, fear etched on his features. One shot. Another. All six. Foss, his body ripped by the imaginary cartridges that Sutton, in his mind, had just fired, lay lifeless on the floor, the red river of his life bursting its banks and ebbing away.

Sutton holstered his .44 and lay down with his back against the bale as he had done before the arrival of Mei-ling and let his imagination roam. A thin smile spread across his features.

Not much longer now, he thought. It's about over. Soon will be. He recalled the vow of vengeance he had made to his dead brother, heard his own words now echoing in the tunnel of time on their way back to him although they had never really left him, had never faded very far from his consciousness.

Beaumont's dead, Dan, Sutton said silently. So's Jim Hawkins. Johnny Loud Thunder too. Adam Foss will be dead before much longer, Dan. Dead as a doornail.

His thoughts continued to wander through the recent years as he recalled the places he had been and the people he had met while he stalked the killers who had robbed him of the best friend he had ever had, his own brother, and when his thoughts finally strayed from the trail and drifted away, Sutton realized that night had come.

He got up and leaped down from the bale. He went out into the pressroom and then into the office which was still empty. He left it and went outside where he walked, without haste, but purposefully, in the direction of Harding's—no, he corrected himself—Foss's house.

Just before he reached it, he spotted the man with the rifle standing on the stoop just outside the front door. So Foss figures me to do exactly what I am doing, he thought. He cut between the house and its nearest neighbor and a second man, who also cradled a rifle in his arms, came into view. He looked up. Windows, just above the roof that slanted above the back porch. A light in one. The other—dark. He looked down and found what he had hoped to find—a rock. He backtrailed until he had reached the middle of the house and looked up again, this time at the roof of the house which sloped up to its peak.

He threw the rock, underhanded, and watched its passage through the light cast by the crescent moon. He watched it sail low over the peak of the roof and then heard it strike the roof on the opposite side and clatter down it.

"Who's there?" the man in front of the house bellowed.

"That you, Crane?" came an answering call from the rear of the house.

Sutton ran back the way he had come but the man at the rear door had not deserted his post. He ran back through the shadows to the front of the house and was relieved to find that the rifleman was gone from the front door.

He sprinted up to it, gun drawn, and turned the knob. The door was locked. He knocked on it, his eyes darting to the right and left because he expected the guard with the rifle to return to his post at any moment.

"Is that you out there, Mr. Crane?" a woman's voice called out from behind the door.

Not Opal's voice, Sutton thought, and said, "Open up."

Nothing happened. Sutton was about to knock again. But then the door opened and the maid Sutton had seen on his earlier visit appeared, a lamp held high in her hand.

"Sir?" she said.

Sutton pushed past her and closed the door behind him. "Where can I find Mr.—" he almost said "Foss" but caught himself in time "—Harding? Got to talk to him. Matter of life and death—his."

The maid, frightened now and showing it, pointed to paneled doors visible at the end of a short hall. "There. He's in the sitting room."

Sutton strode down the hall, unholstering his gun as he did so and ignoring the gasp from the maid behind him. He spun around as he heard a knock on the front door. He flattened himself against the wall and then took up a position behind a tall highboy. "Tell whoever's out there to stay out there," he ordered the maid.

"Everything alright in there, Melinda?" he heard one of the guards ask as the maid opened the front door.

"Yes," she answered abruptly and slammed the door in her haste to close it.

Sutton sprinted down the hall and threw open the paneled doors.

"What—"

"Evening, Foss," Sutton said to the man who had half risen from a Morris chair and remained frozen in that awkward position as he stared up at Sutton.

"You!"

"Me. We meet again for—what's this? The fourth time, if I'm not miscalculating. The *last* time, Foss."

Sutton crossed the room and put a hand on Foss's shoulder,

pushing him down into the Morris chair. "Now, you get your maid in here. I'm going to stand behind this chair of yours with my gun in hand. You know I can kill you right through this chair you're sitting in if you don't do exactly what I say. Tell the maid to send your two guards home. Tell her you'll not be needing them anymore tonight. Or her either. You got any other hired help around this place?"

"A cook."

"Tell the maid to send in the other servants," Sutton ordered.

"There's only the cook."

"Tell her what I just said."

"Pull that bell rope over there," Foss said and Sutton reached out and yanked it.

The maid entered the sitting room a moment later, fear paling her face.

Foss gave her the orders Sutton had dictated to him and she hurried from the room. Minutes later, two men and a woman appeared in the open doorway.

Sutton caught Foss's crestfallen expression which was reflected in a mirror on the other side of the room as Foss dismissed the trio for the night.

"Only a cook, huh?" Sutton snapped when they had gone. "Who were those men?"

Foss remained silent.

Sutton reached out, seized a handful of Foss's hair, and jerked his head backward.

"The butler," Foss said. "The butler and the houseboy."

"You lie easier than a spring rain falls from the sky," Sutton declared, releasing his hold on Foss. "Now, get up and let's go."

"Where?"

"Move!" Sutton followed Foss out of the room and through the house, his gun pressed against the small of Foss's back, as he checked to make sure the house was empty.

It wasn't.

Responding to Sutton's order, Foss opened a door when they reached the second floor to reveal Opal seated at her dressing table, her left arm in a muslin sling.

"Evening," Sutton said to her. "Want to return this to you." He pulled the derringer from his waistband and held it out to her.

She took it, saying nothing, her eyes on him.

"You'd best stay right here in your room," Sutton warned her.

Still she said nothing.

Sutton moved Foss out into the hall and, once they were back in the sitting room, he ordered Foss to sit down in the Morris chair again.

"I hope your wife heeds my advice and stays put in her room up there," he remarked.

"Why?"

"I'd hate like hell having her see what I'm going to do to you, Foss."

CHAPTER 10

Sutton and Foss were silent as they stared steadily at one another.

But the room in which Foss sat and Sutton stood was not.
It whispered of wealth. The crystal decanter and glasses on
the richly inlaid table, the ornate oriental rug covering the
floor, the velvet drapes on the windows, the polished marble

fireplace—all spoke in subdued but unmistakable tones of a life lived well because the one who lived it was rich.

The neatly engraved plaque hanging on the wall above the fireplace, which commended Roy Harding for his "untiring service to Virginia City," spoke of power and prestige.

Sutton heard the voices, all so soft but their message unambiguous, and felt nothing but contempt for them. His voice, when he spoke, silenced them.

"The gunman you sent to Carson City after me—you been wondering what happened to him?" When Foss didn't answer, Sutton said, "He's dead. So is Mercer and I reckon you know that Tulley is too."

He walked over and sat down in a wing chair facing Foss, his gun still in his hand and aimed at Foss. "I figured out how you knew I was in Carson City. It was that story Bill Wright printed in the *Territorial Enterprise* that put you on to me, wasn't it—the one about me winning that shooting contest we had down there?"

"I don't know what you're talking about."

Sutton leaned forward in the chair. "Yes, you do. You sent that man to kill me after you'd read about me in the paper. I got your name from him. I take it, since he knew your real name, you and him'd been traveling the same trail together for some time. Otherwise, he'd have known you as Harding."

"I didn't kill your brother."

"A long time ago, I stopped wondering which one of the four of you actually did it. A long time ago, I decided that, as far as I was concerned, you all did it."

"Did what?" Opal asked from the doorway.

Sutton sighed. "Thought I told you to stay put."

"Did what?" she repeated.

"This man you married's a murderer. You didn't know that, did you?"

Opal seemed to draw into herself but she didn't move.

Sutton told her about the night nearly three years ago—his account of it brief, his words clipped.

"That's the truth, Luke?" Opal asked when he finished.

"It's a lie!" Foss cried. "He's lying!"

Opal's eyes left Sutton's and swung to her husband's face. "Roy, did you help to kill Dan Sutton?"

Before Foss could reply, Sutton said, "His name's not Roy Harding. His name's Adam Foss."

"He's lying!" Foss exclaimed again.

"Why would he lie about a thing like this?" Opal asked, studying her husband.

"Fact is, I wouldn't," Sutton stated quietly. "Wouldn't have a reason in the world to."

"Luke," Opal said, her voice barely audible, "why did you come here tonight?"

"To kill him." Sutton's gaze was on Foss.

"If you do, Luke, you'll be a killer—as you say he is. They'll arrest you for murder. They'll hang you."

"They won't. Once he's dead, I'll be gone. Just like I was after the other three died once I'd caught up with each one of them."

"You killed the others?" Opal's eyes narrowed.

Foss's eyes widened and his fingers gripped the armrests of the Morris chair.

"They're dead," was Sutton's blunt response.

Opal suddenly and swiftly crossed the room, passing Sutton, to stand beside her husband's chair. "Don't do it, Luke. It's not that I have any love—even any least little feeling left —for—for him." She looked down at Foss. "But if you—"

She was unable to finish her sentence because Foss reached up and pulled her toward him while, at the same time, he rose rapidly to his feet. Holding Opal in front of him with both hands, he began to laugh.

Sutton muttered an oath and sprang from his chair.

Foss, from behind Opal, said, "You shouldn't go around giving derringers to strangers, my dear. It can be a dangerous pastime. Tell her that's so, Sutton. The sheriff, when he sent word to me about your escape, said that you'd somehow managed to acquire a derringer. I didn't know until a little while ago how you had managed to get one. Opal, you are a conniving little vixen! I should have sprained more than your wrist when I found out about you and Sutton. I should have broken it and maybe one or two other bones in your admittedly lovely body at the same time."

"Let her go, Foss. She's not part of this. This is between you and me."

Foss forced Opal to move with him toward the far wall. He halted at a writing desk that stood there and, with one hand, he opened its top drawer and removed a .32 caliber revolver which he aimed at Sutton.

"Now the odds are a bit more to my liking. Sutton, I'll make a deal with you. I'll pay you whatever you want if you'll leave here and never come back."

"No deal, Foss. Your offer's a filthy one. You're asking me to put a price on my brother's life."

"I'll throw in this lady as part of the bargain," Foss countered with a smile. "You like her, don't you? I know she likes you because she's been looking out for your interests lately and doing a pretty fair job of it too. You could use her—take her with you—couldn't you?"

Sutton's lips formed a thin line. He said nothing.

"Let me go!" Opal demanded, trying to free herself. "You're hurting my wrist."

"Throw your gun down, Sutton," Foss demanded. "Throw it over here."

When Sutton remained motionless, Foss snarled, "You can't get me, not with Opal shielding me. But you might get her if you try anything. Now, you wouldn't want that to happen, would you?"

Sutton's hand remained on his .44.

Foss swore. "Then she gets it first, Sutton." He placed the barrel of his gun against Opal's temple.

"Don't!" Opal cried, struggling to free herself. "Oh, please don't!"

"You wouldn't do it, Foss," Sutton said in a low tone, not really believing his words but hoping.

"I assure you that I would, Sutton. Now, your gun. Throw it over here."

There was a knocking on the front door. Hurried. Loud.

"*Sutton!*" Foss practically shouted.

Sutton withdrew his finger from his gun's trigger and then tossed the gun across the room.

It landed close to Foss's feet and he quickly bent and scooped it up, releasing Opal at the same time. He thrust his .32 in the desk drawer and closed it. "Answer the door, Opal," he commanded.

Opal was trying to replace the sling which had slipped from her arm when Foss seized her.

He reached out and gave her a vicious shove which sent her stumbling away from him.

She would have fallen but Sutton reached out, caught her, and steadied her.

She looked up at him briefly and then made her way out of the sitting room and down the hall as the knocking increased in intensity.

Sutton, at the sound of the front door opening, looked over his shoulder and saw the sheriff framed in the doorway. He could hear the muted sounds of the man's conversation with Opal and he watched Opal admit the man before again turning his attention to Foss.

"Mr. Harding," the sheriff said as he entered the sitting room. "Something's come up. I had to talk to you. What—" His eyes dropped to Sutton's gun in Foss's hand.

"The man standing there with his back to you, Sheriff," Foss said, "is the man who escaped from your jail earlier today."

"Well, I'll be damned!" the sheriff exclaimed as he stepped forward and recognized Sutton. "You caught him for me."

"And welcome you are to him, Sheriff," Foss said. "Get him out of here—now."

As the sheriff drew his revolver and held it trained on Sutton, Foss put Sutton's gun down on the table next to the crystal decanter and the glasses flanking it.

"Mr. Harding, I'll take him back to the jail but first—"

Sutton said, "That man's not Roy Harding, Sheriff. His name's Adam Foss and him and three other men killed my brother nearly three years ago and shot me up pretty bad at the same time."

"Don't pay any attention to him, Sheriff," Foss said.

"Foss is a murderer," Sutton stated emphatically. "I've been trailing him all this time. He sent a man down to Carson City to try to kill me. He was going to kill me just now when you showed up."

"Adam Foss," the sheriff said and glanced at Foss. "That's funny, that is."

Sutton shifted his position slightly and realized that Opal had not returned. "What's funny about it, Sheriff?"

"I've got a man outside," the sheriff said. "At least, I think he's outside." He backed up, keeping his gun trained on Sutton. "Croft!" he yelled. "You out there? Come on in here if you are."

Croft. The name was familiar to Sutton but at first he couldn't place it. And then, as the man the sheriff had summoned entered the sitting room, he recognized both the man and the name.

"Who is this man?" Foss demanded brusquely.

"You don't remember me?" Croft asked him, turning his hat in his hands. "I guess I'm not the kind of man most people remember. But I remember you and how you cheated me by selling me that worthless claim you salted with silver two years ago. Oh, I remember you, alright."

As Foss frowned in irritation, his eyebrows nearly met his nose. "I don't know you."

The sheriff said, "Mr. Harding, this man—his name's Lester Croft—he came to my office tonight and told me a story I just couldn't believe but he insisted I come over here and check it out."

"What story?" Foss asked, his voice strained.

"Croft claimed that Sutton here went to see him in Carson City because he'd found out somehow that you'd sold him a worthless claim some two years ago. He says that Sutton called you Roy Harding but Croft claims your real name's Adam Foss."

"Why that's preposterous!" Foss bellowed. "Get Sutton out of my house, Sheriff. That other man as well!"

"Now, just hold on a minute, Mr.—whatever your real name is," the sheriff responded.

Croft said to Sutton, "After you went, I decided you were right and maybe I ought to try to get back the money Foss cheated me out of."

"Sheriff," Sutton said, "the man you know as Roy Harding is Adam Foss. Croft's just identified him. I'm identifying him. He's a murderer, like I told you. It's him you want in your jail, not me."

"This is nothing more than a scheme to ruin me," Foss declared, regaining some of his lost composure. "Surely you can see that, Sheriff. Croft told you that he met with Sutton in Carson City. They hatched this scheme at that meeting to besmirch my good name and get their hands on my money." Foss took a silk handkerchief from his pocket and wiped his forehead. "Get them both out of here. I have no time for this nonsense." He pulled an Ingersoll watch from his vest pocket and looked at it. "I'm long overdue at a meeting of the Mine Owners' Association which is being held at Dave Honeywell's home."

"Well, I don't know which way is up and which one down

at the moment and that's a fact," the bewildered sheriff said. "Sutton, I'm going to take you back to jail. Croft, you come along and write down a statement for me. I'll check this whole thing out in the morning."

"Excuse me, Sheriff," Foss said and hurriedly left the room.

Croft groaned. "I'll never nail him," he muttered. "A rich man like Foss'll always be able to get away with whatever dirty tricks he pulls."

"Sheriff," Sutton said, watching Foss climb the stairs to the second floor, "you're making a mistake. Foss won't be here in the morning. Now that I've run him to ground, he wants me back in jail so he can make his getaway. He'll be gone by morning—or soon after. I'll guarantee it."

"Let's go, Sutton. Maybe you're right and maybe you're wrong. We'll find out starting tomorrow."

Sutton turned and started for the door. As he came abreast of the sheriff, he thrust out one booted foot and, when it hooked behind the sheriff's ankles, he jerked it forward.

The sheriff lost his balance. His hands swung up into the air.

Sutton grabbed the sheriff's wrist and ripped the gun from the man's hand. "*Croft!*" he said sharply. "You and me are going to both be out of luck if I don't get my hands on Foss. Take this gun and—"

"No," Croft said nervously. "I'm no gunfighter."

"Take it, Croft, and hold it on the sheriff here. Don't let him make a move. I'm going after Foss."

Croft reluctantly took the sheriff's gun Sutton handed him and, as he did so, Sutton retrieved his own gun from the table where Foss had placed it earlier and then sprinted from the room and up the stairs to the second floor.

He threw open the first door he came to and found the room beyond it empty. The next door he opened proved to be a storage closet. Opal, he thought. Maybe Foss is with her.

He ran down the hall to the door of Opal's bedroom which, when he discovered it was locked, he promptly booted open.

Foss was inside the room, his hand thrust deep into the recesses of a wall safe he had opened. Opal stood motionless in a corner of the room, alarm on her face as she stared in silence at Sutton.

"Foss!"

Foss, also staring at Sutton, stood as motionless as his wife and, for a moment, none of the three people in the room moved.

But then Sutton raised his .44.

Foss withdrew his hand from the safe and in it was a snub-nosed Colt which he fired at Sutton.

But Sutton had ducked down behind an upholstered chair and the bullet missed him and then he quickly rose, prepared to fire.

A shot rang out. It had come from the main floor of the house. It was followed almost immediately by the sound of boots thudding up the stairs.

Foss leaped to one side and seized Opal around the waist. In one swift movement, he hurled her across the room to smash into the chair behind which Sutton stood. She toppled it and it, in turn, sent Sutton crashing to the floor.

Foss bounded forward until he reached Sutton. He kicked the gun from Sutton's hand and squeezed the trigger of his own gun a moment later.

An instant before the shot roared in the room, Sutton rolled to one side and came up with his gun in his hand.

"Hold it!" the sheriff shouted from the bedroom doorway, his revolver in his hand. "Drop your guns, you two!"

Foss was the first to obey the order.

Then Sutton tossed his .44 onto a chair.

"He came gunning for me, Sheriff," Foss said. "You got here just in time and I can't tell you how grateful I am that you did."

"You say he came gunning for you," the sheriff said. "Maybe he did. But it looked to me like you were gunning for him too."

"I had to defend myself, Sheriff," Foss protested, his voice bordering on a whine.

"Sutton," the sheriff said, gesturing with his gun. And then he fell as the wooden chair in the hands of Croft, who had crept up behind him in the hall, came crashing down upon his head.

"He got the jump on me downstairs," Croft said to Sutton. "Told you I was no gunfighter."

Sutton missed Croft's words as he sprang for the two guns —his own and Foss's.

Foss jumped him before he reached them and both men went down.

They rolled over, Sutton losing his hat as he struggled to free his right arm in order to deliver a punch, Foss battling to get his hands around Sutton's throat.

Foss, on top of Sutton as both men hit the wall, got one hand on Sutton's throat. With his free hand, he reached for his gun which lay not far away.

He almost had it when Sutton brought both of his knees up to catch Foss in his midsection. He arched his back and managed to place his boots against Foss's gut. He shoved hard and Foss went flying away from him to crash into the upholstered chair that lay on its side in the middle of the room.

Foss scrambled around the chair and found his gun. Crouching behind the chair, he took aim at Sutton.

Opal sprang forward, reaching for Foss's gun.

Foss turned his gun on her, cursing, and was about to pull the trigger when a shot rang out.

Sutton stared in surprise as Foss fell to the floor and blood poured from his left temple.

Opal stood with her back to Sutton. Croft was standing

wide-eyed and openmouthed in the doorway. Beside him, the sheriff was getting to his feet and groggily shaking his head.

What had happened, Sutton asked himself.

Opal turned toward him, her face expressionless.

Sutton looked down at the derringer in her right hand, the one she had given to Mei-ling to give to him and which he had returned to her less than an hour ago. He looked up at her face, at the coldness of her eyes and the set line of her jaw.

"He would have killed me," she said, but she did not seem to be speaking to Sutton or to anyone else. "He beat me. More than once." She looked down at her arm which was still in its sling. "He sprained my wrist the last time he came after me." She sighed, a mournful sound in the quiet room. She looked down at the unmoving body of her husband. "It's strange. I thought I would feel—happy once I'd killed him. I don't. I feel—nothing." She glanced at Sutton, a sense of wonder in her eyes.

Sutton missed her glance because he was staring down at Foss and listening to the echo of Opal's words. He's dead, he thought. I don't feel happy about that fact any more than Opal does. I feel— He searched for the right word. Glad? No. Relieved? A little. And then he knew what it was that he was feeling. He was feeling *free*.

Croft whistled through his teeth. "She pulled that derringer out of that sling she'd hid it in faster than frost kills."

Sutton, staring at Foss's body, suddenly stiffened.

Had it really happened? Had he actually seen what he thought he had seen? He took a tentative step toward Foss.

Foss's eyes opened. They tried to focus. "Su—" he hissed. Blood, mixed with saliva, slid from one corner of his mouth.

Sutton moved forward and then got down on one knee beside Foss. Without looking away from the man's glazed eyes, he beckoned to the sheriff who came up to stand beside him.

"—s true. Killed . . . your brother, Su—"

Sutton gripped Foss's shoulder and squeezed it roughly. "What's your name?" he muttered harshly.

Foss's head fell to one side.

Using the barrel of his .44 which was still in his hand, Sutton turned Foss's head so that he faced the ceiling again. "Who are you?" he demanded.

"Adam—" One of Foss's eyes opened but only partially. "*Fosssss*," he said.

And died.

Sutton looked up at the sheriff.

"Told you so, Sheriff," Croft murmured.

Opal sobbed once and turned away.

Sutton stood up and holstered his gun. "You heard him, Sheriff."

"I heard him. Seems like you and Croft here were telling the truth about him—who he is and what he done."

"I was."

"It looks like I wind up a loser again," Croft remarked dolefully. "With Foss dead, I stand no chance to sue for what's due me."

"I'll repay you for the way my husband cheated you, Mr. Croft," Opal said, turning to face the three men again. "I know what he did to you. He bragged openly about it often enough." Dry-eyed now, she said, "Sheriff, I killed him in self-defense."

The sheriff nodded. "I saw what happened. You did what you had to do, I guess."

Sutton said, "About that Texas lawman who's on his way to get his hands on me, Sheriff. I reckon you'll tell him what happened here when he gets here and about who really killed my brother. About who that man really is." Sutton pointed to Foss's corpse. "I'd be obliged if you would so that my name can be cleared at last."

"I'll do that. It's a pity, though."

Sutton glanced questioningly at the sheriff as he picked up his hat and put it on.

"It's a pity that I don't have Foss to turn over to that lawman who's traveling all the way up here from Texas. Seems a shame to send him home empty-handed."

"I'll be going," Sutton said and started for the door.

Before he reached it, an explosion resounded in the night outside, rattling the windows of the bedroom and causing the chandelier that hung from the ceiling to sway slightly.

"What the hell was that?" the sheriff asked, startled.

Sutton went to the window and looked out. "Dynamite," he said, "or I miss my guess. Something's burning up on Mount Davidson."

Opal appeared at his side. "That's the hoisting works of the Golden Mine." She gasped. "Look, Luke!"

Sutton saw what Opal had seen and pointed out to him.

Men, silhouetted against the flames, ran in every direction as a fire blazed around them. Soldiers appeared. Rifles were raised. The sound of shooting shattered the night.

"The militiamen," Opal cried. "They're attacking the strikers!"

"Maybe it's the other way round," Sutton commented. "Either way, it means trouble." He suddenly remembered Foss mentioning the meeting of the Mine Owners' Association. He turned to Opal. "What're your feelings about what the miners want where wages and working conditions are concerned?"

"My feelings? Why, I—I don't know really. I've never given such matters much thought. My husband always—"

"Give them some thought," Sutton interrupted. "Now."

"Luke, I can't just—one doesn't make up one's mind about such important matters at a moment's notice."

"Come on!" he said and seized her hand. He ran past Croft and the sheriff, practically dragging Opal behind him, remembering the promise he had made to Jack Penrose.

"Luke! Slow down!" Opal ran behind him. Out of the room. Down the stairs. Out of the house.

Sutton didn't slow down. He ran through the streets with Opal, her hair coming undone as she struggled to keep up with him.

When he reached Honeywell's house, he sprinted up to the front door and pounded on it. When it didn't open immediately in response to his knock, he opened it and pulled Opal inside. "*Honeywell!*"

Honeywell appeared in the hall, an expression of surprise that bordered on alarm on his face.

"Honeywell, there's a battle going on at the Golden Mine between the strikers and the militiamen. I got the impression when you and me talked before that you wouldn't mind giving the men who worked for you a raise and maybe improve the conditions they work under."

"Harding—" Honeywell managed to get out with an apologetic glance in Opal's direction.

"Harding's dead!" Sutton said quickly. "Mrs. Harding'll be taking over for him. She's agreed to raise her miners' pay to four dollars a day." He glanced almost fiercely at Opal.

She nodded assent.

Sutton quickly outlined other changes he claimed Opal had decided to make in the High Stakes Mine. He looked at her again. She nodded again. "So, Honeywell, what about you? You'll go along now that Harding's no longer got his claws into you?"

"Yes," said Honeywell decisively.

"What about the other owners?" Sutton prodded.

"Excuse me." Honeywell disappeared and, when he reappeared a few minutes later, he was smiling. "Mr. Sutton, we've all agreed to match the changes Mrs. Harding's planning to make at the High Stakes."

"Good!" Sutton said. "Opal, you stay here and catch your breath."

He was almost out the door when Opal called to him. "Where are you going, Luke?"

"To dampen down the hellfire those men are stoking up there on Mount Davidson!"

He sprinted toward the flames rising high above the buildings in the distance, his breath hammering its way out of his burning lungs. He coughed as he inadvertently swallowed acrid smoke.

He raced up the slope of Mount Davidson toward the shouting men whose faces were now red, now black, depending upon the direction in which the wind sent the flames flowing.

Occasional rifle shots sounded.

Swearing men ran past Sutton.

He picked his target and headed for it on the run. When he reached the filled ore cart, he leaped up on top of it and let out a yell, his hands cupped around his mouth, his head thrown back. His wordless yell was a wild roaring in the noisy night, dwarfing the other sounds around him.

At first, nothing happened.

Sutton looked down as another explosion ripped a storage building apart and saw the cluster of men who were reloading a makeshift catapult they had constructed. He leaped down from the ore cart and raced toward it. He flung the men aside, tearing from their hands the beer bottles they held which they had filled with blasting caps and sticks of dynamite, intending to launch them toward the ragged line of militiamen in the distance.

When one miner swung a fist at him, he knocked the man to the ground and again let out a yell.

This time it produced relative quiet in which only the murmuring of curious men and the crackling of flames could be heard. He ran back to the ore cart and jumped up on it. He held up both arms and yelled, "Listen to me!"

He waited, the firelight bathing his sweating body, until the men had quieted and begun to gather around the ore cart. When he saw the militiamen rise from their knees and place the stocks of their rifles against the ground, he called out, "The strike's over!"

"Like hell it is!" a miner shouted back.

"Shut your mouth, mister!" Sutton shouted at the man. "Now, all of you, listen to me." He quickly outlined the concessions the mine owners were willing to make to the strikers.

When he had finished, someone shouted, "How do we know what you say is true?"

"You can check it for yourselves," Sutton replied. "You know where Mr. Honeywell lives. He's there now along with the other members of the Mine Owners' Association. I just talked to him. You send a delegation over there and ask him if what I said is true."

"We'll do that!" the man who had questioned Sutton declared. "Come on, boys!"

"What about the ice chamber?" someone called out.

"From now on it's to be fifteen minutes of work and then fifteen minutes off in the ice chamber. No more half-hour work stints."

The crowd around the ore cart was silent. And then, as if an understanding of their victory had suddenly descended upon them, a cheer went up into the night to lose itself among the stars in the sky overhead. It was quickly followed by another and then the crowd quickly began to dissolve.

Less than five minutes later, Sutton found himself alone.

The militiamen had vanished. So had the crowd.

He climbed down from the ore cart and wearily wiped the sweat from his face. He began to walk down the mountain but he had not gone very far when a shadow detached itself from a pool of still deeper shadows and stepped in front of him.

"Bill," Sutton said as he recognized Wright. "You're here for a story I take it."

Wright nodded. "You won the battle, I see. Congratulations!"

For an instant, Sutton saw Jack Penrose's smiling face before him and then it ghosted away into the night.

"What's Harding—I mean Foss—going to say to all this, Luke?"

"Nothing. He's dead."

Wright started to ask a question but then, seeing the stern expression on Sutton's face, thought better of it. He reached into his pocket and took something from it which he handed to Sutton.

Sutton took it and looked down at the carved piece of jade he held in his hand.

"Just before I put Mei-ling and her grandfather on the stage to San Francisco," Wright said, "she gave me this to give to you."

Sutton raised his hand and studied the jade. It was circular and slightly smaller than a silver dollar. The firelight flickered on it, seeming to make the female figure carved on its surface undulate.

"What is it?" Sutton asked, looking up at Wright.

"Mei-ling told me to tell you that the lady carved on that jade is someone she called the Maiden Immortal. Mei-ling said she is one of the Eight Immortals who live on the Three Isles of the Blessed. That peach the lady's carrying in her hand—"

Sutton looked down at it.

"—is a symbol of immortality. Mei-ling said to tell you that she will pray to the Maiden Immortal and ask her to protect you in the days to come."

Sutton put out his right hand and shook hands with Wright. "I've got to be moving on now, Bill. It's been good knowing you."

Wright silently clapped Sutton on the shoulder and remained where he was as Sutton made his way down the mountain.

Behind him, Sutton heard one of the burning buildings col-
lapse. He didn't look back at it. They'll start rebuilding tomorrow, he thought, now that things have changed for the
better for them the way they have for me too. I've got
some rebuilding of my own to do, he reminded himself and,
as he did so, exultation swept through him, washing away his
weariness, and he couldn't help himself. He threw back his
head and howled his happiness into the night—the happiness
that came from his strong sense of being once again a man
free to live his life in his own way wherever he might choose
to do so.

He pocketed the piece of jade that depicted the Maiden
Immortal and walked on through the night toward the new
day that was waiting for him.

ABOUT THE AUTHOR

Leo P. Kelley has written more than a dozen novels and published many short stories in leading magazines. In addition to the four Luke Sutton books, he has written a suspense novel, *Deadlocked!*, which was nominated for the Mystery Writers of America's Edgar Award.